TAKING CHANCES

KIM SMART

This is entirely a work of fiction. All people, places, and events contained herein have been completely fabricated by the author. Any similarities to real people, places, or events are entirely coincidental.

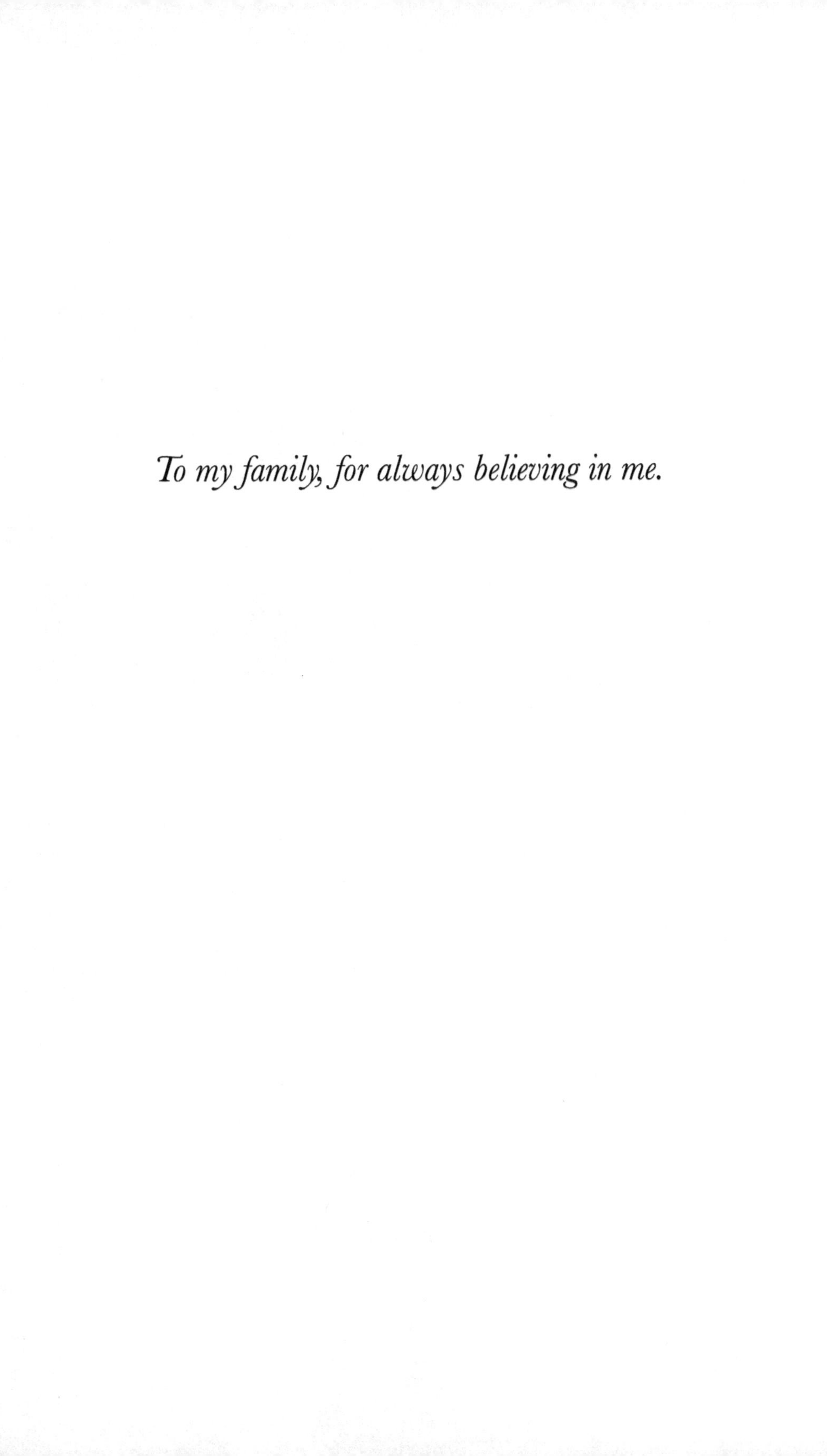

To my family, for always believing in me.

CONTENTS

1
___

ig Brutus, the rankest bull in this circuit, writhes beneath him, trapped in the bucking chute with two hundred pounds of determined man sitting on his ornery one-ton body. The bull's instincts urge him to fling that nuisance off his back. The chute handler rubs a rope under the bull's neck to distract him. Chance nods for the gate to open. Dust flies as Big Brutus kicks high and to the right.

Images come to him as he lies in the darkness trying to put the pieces together. That's all he remembers from his last ride. He's not even sure he made it eight seconds. Distant voices fill the void before he sees them; the voices of his mother and father. It hurt to open his eyes. It hurt to breathe. He just flippin' hurt.

Screams commanding silence reverberate in his head.

The noise, beeping and air moving, something tightening around his arm. What kind of hell is this? Her voice, just above a whisper, grates on him. His jaw tenses as he tries to close his ears. He wants to open his mouth but it's glued shut, his tongue stuck to the roof. He falls back to sleep. Too tired to fight through the confusion… and the pain.

"IT'S so peaceful on the trail. Nobody and nothing to tell me what to do. Honestly, I would rather deal with the predators on the trail than bill collectors in town." Stella's parents really didn't understand her lifestyle, even though they had ranched all their lives. Unless one was a northern Arizona high desert rancher, you probably couldn't understand. It's a very different life when you sleep under the stars with your livestock. Most ranchers spend their nights on a soft mattress, away from the elements.

That voice. Stella? Is that her? He tried to open his mouth again. With perseverance he frees his tongue and wets his lips. His mouth feels like a dry, gritty sandbox.

"Can…" his voice came out a whisper. He inhaled, steeling himself against the pain in his chest. His eyelids fluttered, shielding his eyes from the bright light overhead. "C-Can you kids hold it down? I'm trying to rest over here."

"Chancey! Oh, Chancey! There you are." His mother, Yvette, rushed to the bed and took his free hand in hers.

"Um, no! I come a thousand miles to see you and all you do is sleep. No, I won't be quiet." Stella smiled down at her brother. The corners of his mouth turned slightly.

Chance swallowed hard. "Did anyone get the license plate number?"

He looked to his dad, Dan, who smiled back at him. "Yes, it was B-R-U-T-U-S."

Dan reached out to pat his son's shoulder. His hand stopped mid-air. "Son, where don't you hurt?" Dan was no stranger to cowboy accidents. He was sure his boy was hurting, especially since the doctors lightened his sedation.

"Now that's a good question. My butt's numb, so maybe there?" Chance bent his left leg and pressed his foot into the bed to reposition his hips. His face curled into itself in pain. "Ah, no, that hurts too."

"What the heck happened? I remember being on Brutus, coming out the gate and that's about it. Where am I?" Chance could see he was in a hospital but didn't know where the hospital was.

"You're at Bellsville Hospital, honey." Yvette turned to see if she could get the attention of a nurse outside the glass Intensive Care Unit door. "Would you like a sip of water?"

She wasn't sure if he could have any, but dry skin hung from his lips and she ached to bring him some relief. He had only had intravenous fluids for the nearly four days he was unconscious.

"Bellsville? Now how on earth did I get here?" Chance looked around the room, trying to make sense of his situation.

"Well, what have we here?" A doctor walked in, rubbing disinfectant gel over her hands. She was mid-thirties, pretty, and had been very attentive to Chance's condition during his stay. "Hello. I'm Dr. Carmichael. You, sir, have been through a lot. Can you tell me who you are?"

Chance looked to his mom. "Martin Alvarez," he responded, straight-faced. The confused doctor looked to the family for input.

Yvette smiled and shook her head. Her son the jokester hadn't lost it. "Oh, son. Be nice to the good doctor. She's been working hard to protect that brain of yours. Show her you still have one."

Chance looked up to the doctor. "I'm sorry, ma'am, and thank you for protecting my pea brain. I'm Chance Michael Davies, pleased to meet you." He held out his hand to shake hers.

"Well, Mr. Chance Davies, you are one lucky bull rider. It seems that Big… What was his name?"

"The bull was Big Brutus ma'am. Rankest bull I ever met."

"That's right. Big Brutus. Well, Big Brutus wanted to take you out in a big way. Can I give you a rundown of what's been going on with you? Are you awake enough to hear this?"

"Yes ma'am. I think I'd like to know what's creating all this hurt in me." Chance adjusted himself in bed again and held his hand over his eyes to shield them from the light. "First, would it be okay if we turn the lights down? My head is about to explode."

A nurse walked in just then to check on Chance. She turned the lights out as she passed the switch.

"Here's the thing. When you came to us, you were unconscious. That Big Brutus, he knocked your head pretty good. You had some serious swelling in your brain and we were about this close…" Dr. Carmichael held her thumb and forefinger out, showing a sliver of space between them. "…to needing surgery to give your brain more room to swell. There's been a lot of swelling in there, and some bleeding, but we slowed it down enough with medication and rest so that we didn't have to make a hole in your head."

Chance rubbed his hand across his head. "So, no funny haircuts?" He smiled at the doctor.

"That's right. No funny haircuts from us. Now, you're not out of the woods yet. Like I said, there was some bleeding and there is still a very slow leak. We are watching it to make sure it doesn't get worse and we expect it will stop on its own." She paused to let him absorb that information and ask questions.

"Well, is that it? That doesn't sound so bad." Chance knew there was more. His body told him so.

"Well, I'm sure you've noticed that your left arm is strapped down. You have a couple of things going on in there. First, when you hung up on the bull…" Dr. Carmichael looked at Dan, who had given her a lesson in bull riding lingo "…you tore the muscles attached at your shoulder but then, and we can tell this from the large bruise in that area, Big Brutus stepped on you so you've got some fractures in there, too. We will do some surgery in there but we needed your brain to be more stable first."

"Is it possible old Brutus caught some ribs,

too? I gotta tell you doc, there isn't anything in this body that doesn't hurt right now."

"It is possible, but when we x-rayed your chest, we saw old fractures." She paused and looked from Chance to his parents. "Lots of old fractures. If a new break happened in one of those old healed areas, we may not pick it up, so if you say your ribs hurt I believe you. There is nothing displaced in your chest. There isn't a rib that's broken and will poke your heart or your lungs, so you know that it just takes time for the pain to go away."

"Okay. Got it. Is that it?"

"No Chance, not quite. You probably noticed that you have a brace on your neck and you can't really move your head around much. That's because you have some fractures in your cervical spine." Dr. Carmichael pointed to the vertebrae along the back of her neck. "In this area here."

"Really? I think that's a first for me."

"I think so too, because we didn't see any signs of old fractures there. Once again, you got lucky. The vertebrae did not move. There are seven cervical vertebrae. Numbers four, five and six show fractures, but your spinal cord is in good shape. What we will need to do is keep a collar on." Dr. Carmichael reached over and tapped on the plastic of the collar. "This one is called a semirigid collar. It's meant to stop you from moving your head around. As those fractures show some healing, we can replace this with a soft collar. It's more comfortable."

Dr. Carmichael paused, waiting for questions and gauging Chance's understanding of everything she told him.

"So, I will not want to hang around here too long. I mean, you're really pretty and nice and stuff, but this really isn't my scene. What's next so I can get out of here?"

"I will have the orthopedic surgeon come in and talk to you about repairing your shoulder. We will start some rehab, and after your shoulder surgery we can talk about long-term rehab."

"So, what's wrong with my shoulder again?"

Yvette, Dan and Stella looked from Chance to Dr. Carmichael. They had all heard the same explanation he did. Why didn't he remember?

"Okay Chance. Let me tell you what. I think your brain needs to rest a bit. One thing we see with head injuries is short-term memory problems. I will write a list of things we are treating and I will ask Brenda, the nurse here, to bring you a paper and pen. Can you write with your free hand?"

"Sure. It's the one I use to write with."

"Okay, let's do that and I'm going to look at your pain medicine. Hopefully, the surgeon will be in today to talk to you about your shoulder. Sound good?"

"Sure doc. Hey, did you meet all these people here?"

"I sure did. They've been hanging out here waiting for you to wake up. And this little guy…" Dr. Carmichael put her hand on Marco's dark curls. "He'll be an excellent physician one day."

"Who is he anyway?" Chance looked at Marco. He didn't recognize him. Dr. Carmichael looked to Yvette.

"It's true you never met Marco before. His mom works at the dude ranch and he came with us to watch you ride." Yvette took Marco by the hand and brought him nearer the bed. "He will go back with Jesse soon."

"Oh, thank God. I thought I forgot I had a baby brother or something. Hey little man, it's nice to meet you."

Marco approached Chance's bed and held out his hand. "I'm Marco. It's nice to meet you Chancey."

"Chancey. Now that's funny. I bet this has been a boring trip for you, hasn't it?"

"I will let you guys chat. Chance, try to get some rest. We'll be back to check on you after a while." Dr. Carmichael washed her hands and left the room, sliding the glass door behind her.

"Well, wasn't that fun? She's so cheery giving all that bad news. Something's not right about that."

"Oh Chance, she's good people." Stella noticed her brother fidgeting in bed, trying to get comfortable. "I think we'll step out and let you get some rest. Is that okay with you? And we'll stop by and make sure the nurse is on top of your pain meds, okay?"

"That sounds fantastic." Chance's eyelids were heavy. He could barely keep them open. "Hey Stella, how long can you stay? I might be better company tomorrow."

"I'll be here. I'll sneak you a burger if I can." She gave him a thumbs up on her way out.

"Oh man, that sounds fantastic. See ya." Chance mumbled as he drifted off to sleep.

"Yvette, are you happy?" Marco reached his small hand up to Yvette's as they walked down the sterile corridor.

"Oh yes, Marco! I'm thrilled! Son, we've seen a miracle today. My boy woke up and he was telling jokes just like his old self. It's truly a miracle to see him talking and recognizing us. Now, we just need the doctors to fix his shoulder and then he can come home and get strong again." Yvette swung Marco's hand as they walked to the elevator.

Stella nestled into Dan's side. "I think this calls for a celebration. What do you say we go get some pizza?"

While waiting for dinner, they video chatted with Steve to update him. He was in the dining hall with Bella, so Marco got to see and talk to her. Marco made introductions between Bella and Stella. "Mom, this is my new friend, Stella. Stella, this is my mom. Her name is Bella."

Marco laughed. "Get it? Bella and Stella. They rhyme!"

The laughter felt good to this group who had been through so much over the past few days.

A pro rodeo friend of Chance's, Buck Cortez, visited Chance at the hospital in Bellsville earlier in the day to check in on him. Buck offered to take Jesse back to the arena in

Allentown to get Chance's stuff. Jesse pulled into the RV lot just as the rest of the family returned from dinner. Yvette gave him a full recounting of the day's events at the hospital. "He's so much better than I know he could be with a head injury. I know I've said it a lot, but a miracle has happened here today."

Jesse gave his mom a hug, grateful that she didn't have to face what they all knew in the back of their minds was a possibility. "I sent the horses home with Joe Anderson. He said he could drop them off on his way back to Opal City."

Jesse tugged his boots off and unpacked his sweat pants for sleep. He was physically and emotionally drained from the drive, meeting with the rodeo sponsors and others interested in Chance's condition. "There sure were a lot of people asking about Chance. I guess he has made some fantastic friends on the road."

"Truth be known Jesse, I don't think you can find more humble, caring people than cowboys who live close to the land. And they are that way, not just with people but with their animals, too." Stella was a firm believer in the cowboy way of life.

"The audio-visual crew at the arena made a copy of the video of Jesse's ride and accident for me. I could only stomach about ten seconds after the buzzer went off. I'll hold on to it in case he wants to see it one day. But seriously, I think it's too soon."

"You know he'll want to see it. Thanks for getting that, Jesse." Dan also wanted to see it, but not yet.

For the first time in several days they all slept well in the RV.

2

———————

"Hey Angela, this is Steve Davies from Buffalo Ridge. I work with Bella."

Steve was doing chores at the family homestead. He had sent Bella out to the yard to gather eggs and feed the chickens so he could make this call without her.

"Steve, what's up? Is something wrong with Bella? Marco?" Angela had panic in her voice, unusual for the cool-headed emergency-room nurse. Angela was Bella and Marco's roommate in the big city, before Bella left for an adventure on the ranch far away from gangsters, mobsters and smog.

"No, sorry. Nothing like that."

"Oh, thank goodness. How is your brother?"

"Chance is doing better. In fact, he woke up

14

yesterday. The family is so grateful for the good care he is getting in Bellsville. Thank you so much for talking to me the other night and explaining the medical terminology. That helped so much. It's hard to know what's going on when you don't speak the language."

"You are welcome. I understand what it can be like. Here in Manhattan we have the same issue. People in critical condition but their loved ones are not familiar with basic physiology, let alone the complex medical terms we use." She paused. "So, what can I do for you today?"

"Well, I would like to do something for you, if I can. I was wondering if it would be remotely possible for you to come out for a visit. Kind of a thank you present for Bella. She has done such a fabulous job for me and she has had little time off. I just think a visit from home would be nice. I know she and Marco would both be so thrilled to see you, but I want it to be a surprise."

"Are you kidding me? I would love to come, of course! Let me see if I can get some time off, okay? I need a couple of days to check the schedule."

"Sure, sure. Whatever time you need. But please, don't let her know."

"Got it Steve. Thank you so much for this opportunity. I look forward to meeting you and your family in person. I hear so many wonderful things about you all and the ranch. Will be in touch. I've got to go now…shower and get to work. Spin class was a killer today."

"I look forward to hearing from you Angela."

The next few days were a flurry of activity. Chance continued to improve. Jesse and Marco drove back to Buffalo Ridge. Marco resumed his summer adventures in the greenhouse, riding the lawnmower or checking fences and cattle with Jesse or Steve. Sometimes he hung out in his mom's office, telling stories, coloring and practicing his alphabet.

"Here Steve. I drew a picture for you." Marco was coloring in Bella's office while she prepped food in the kitchen. Steve wandered through often when Bella was there. Initially she thought he was looking for something to eat, but more recently figured out he was coming by just to be around her.

"Wow! Thanks big guy! It looks like these people are having a party." Steve pointed to the stick figures positioned around a rectangle in the middle of the paper.

"That's my birthday party. It's your invitation. Can you come?" Marco pointed out all the people at the party in his picture. Steve was next to Bella; Yvette, Jesse and Stella were there. Dan was late to the party and was still in the pickup truck in the yard.

"Well, when is this big party of yours?" This was the first Steve had heard of Marco's birthday. He reflected on his conversation with Angela a few days earlier. He hadn't heard back from her yet.

From Bella, Steve learned that Marco's birthday was in mid-August. She had not yet looked at the calendar to set a date for the party.

"Well, if there is anything I can do to help let me know."

Steve and Marco exchanged a high-five as Steve headed back to work. He stopped just outside the hall to text Angela. *Just heard Marco's birthday is coming up. Does it work for you to come around that time? Let me know. Steve*

He hoped Angela could be here for Marco's birthday. There was so much he could show her and she could see for herself that they were happy, and how well-adjusted Marco was here. That was important to all of them.

Over the next several days, Steve and Angela exchanged texts, secured airline tickets and established a plan for the big day. She would arrive on Marco's birthday, early enough to take part in the festivities.

Steve and Bella continued to monitor Chance's progress from afar. Yvette and Dan stayed on until he was ready to return home with them. Yvette knew this son was an independent one. It had been many years since he lived at home, under their watchful eye. But being a mom, and the caretaker she was, she wanted her son home.

"Chance, you know we want you to come home with us for your rehab. Your room is ready and your horses are there, but if you think it's not a good idea, if you have somewhere else to be, just let us know."

"Mom, I am thankful for your offer. I've been living out of horse trailers and motel rooms for a long time. It will be nice to wake up in the same bed for over two days in a row. Are you sure you won't get tired of having me around?"

"No way! Now, the doctor will make a referral for rehab and an orthopedic doctor to do the follow-up on your shoulder. I have some feelers out to see who in Buffalo Ridge might know of someone to help with the rehab, but we have no problem taking you to the city to see someone too. Do you think you can make the drive home okay? Dad will drive the RV. You can lie down in there, and I will drive your pickup. Sound good?"

Jesse agreed and two days later, with copies of medical records, dressing supplies and prescriptions filled, they left for Buffalo Ridge. Chance had not been home for any more than a quick hello, while passing through on the nearby interstate, for three years. So much had changed.

It was almost dark when they arrived. The house looked terrific. His mother was a natural in the home economics department. She made everything feel so warm and inviting. Besides ranching and farming, his parents had a rodeo livestock business. That herd had grown. Some beautiful broncos roamed the pastures and the bulls they gained were solid stock for the small and mid-sized rodeos they catered to.

Dan was ready to go to work at sunrise the next morning. Chance was already in the yard when he headed to his pickup. "Morning Pops."

"You're up mighty early, son. Beautiful day out here."

"I tell ya, I've been lying around in that hospital bed long enough. It's time I get outside and put my boots in the dirt. Well I can't really pull my boots on yet with this bum arm, but I found these old sneakers in my closet. I can't believe I still have old stuff in that room. Mom could have thrown all that stuff away."

"Yeah, but I bet you're glad this morning that she didn't. Looks like you found an old shirt to throw over that bum arm, too." Dan recognized an old chambray work shirt Chance left behind once when passing through. He remembered how Yvette had washed and ironed it. He had given her a hard time then about ironing an old work shirt. It looked good on him today.

Chance rode in the pickup while Dan checked the fences and watered the cattle. He needed to be out in the fresh air where he could smell the wild and sit in silence. They dotted their ride with observations about the condition of the fence or the need to spray for thistle. They drove into the far east pasture to check the water trough.

"Hey Dad, isn't that Lucky Len out there? Looks just like him." Jesse rode Lucky Len in his early rodeo days at a stampede in Wyoming. He was a big cream-colored Charbray bull with a mean streak as hot as a timber fire in a drought. Somewhere Chance had some great photos of that bull bucking him high and kicking wide.

"Good eye, son. That's Lucky's grandson. We call him Lookie Lou. He's popular with the cowboys around here. Tame in the field but put him in the chute and he's ready to rock and roll. His circuit days are over now though. We rent him out for Scottie's Riding School. You remember Paul Scotsman?"

"No kidding! Scottie's teaching now, eh? I remember watching him when I was first starting on bulls. He was unbreakable, that guy. Does he ride at all now?"

"Well, kinda like you, he had a pretty bad wreck in Oklahoma on a bad bull. Iron Clad didn't even let him out of the chute before he flipped on him. Crushed his pelvis and some vertebrae, I think. His wife gave him the ultimatum then."

"Dang. Guess I hadn't heard that, or I did and I forgot. That seems to happen a lot to me."

They rode in silence for a few minutes before Dan spoke. "You okay to stop by the dude ranch? I don't think you've been here since I got all the buildings finished, have you?"

"No. Steve sent me a link to the website and it looks great, but last time I was over here was not too long after Vikki passed. Steve was spending a lot of time at the greenhouse."

Chance fell silent again as they drove the five miles to Steve's ranch. Once part of the original homestead, Dan and Yvette had sold it to Steve and his late wife Vikki. Vikki passed away suddenly from leukemia just a few years back. She was an urban organic farmer who established her own greenhouse on the place. She was beautiful and wildly popular in the community.

"How's Steve doing? He looked like a whipped dog the last time I saw him. Long face with those sad eyes."

"He's doing better these days. The dude ranch has been a great outlet for him and it's going strong. One of the best things he did was to bring in Bella, the cook. That's Marco's mom. Crazy story how she came in from Manhattan. Had never been west of the Mississippi before. To hear her tell it, she was locked in that concrete jungle and didn't really see much life outside the city. And you saw that kid of hers; he's brought so much life to the place. Anyway, I think you'll like her. We all do."

Marco saw Dan's pickup coming down the gravel road toward the ranch. He ran to the dude ranch dining hall where his mom was working in the kitchen. "Mom, Dan's coming. Do you have any of that breakfast cake he likes? I'll pour him a cup of coffee."

Marco stretched himself up, reaching to the shelf to get a coffee cup. Dan was predictable and Marco liked to sit with him. One of them was always telling a story.

"Well good morning, Bella!" Dan spoke warmly. "I'd like you to meet another of my boys."

"Chance, it's a pleasure to meet you. I've heard so much about you." Bella nodded to Marco.

"Pleasure, ma'am and I have to say, that's one fine young cowboy you have there. He can spin a yarn as well as old pops here." Chance's free hand thumped his dad in the chest. Bella looked at him quizzically. She hadn't heard that phrase before, but if she was comparing her son to Dan, it had to have something to do with telling a story.

Chance looked Bella over as she walked to the kitchen. "You fellas want some breakfast? The guests went through early. Had to get an early start with the heat index being so high. I've got plenty here for ya."

"Here Dan, I have a cup of coffee for you, with cream, just the way you like it." Marco carefully carried the cup, filled to the brim, to the table and set it in front of Dan. He looked to Chance. "Would you like one Chancey?"

Chance smiled. "Sure son. I like mine black. None of that fancy stuff for me, please." Marco ran to the kitchen to get another cup.

As Chance watched the boy, he caught site

of Bella through the open serving window that separated the dining hall and the kitchen. "Bella's a pretty little thing," he mumbled to his father.

"Yep, she sure is, and has a heart of gold. Hard to believe she didn't grow up here the way she's caught on to things. Steve tells me she was even out taking care of the chickens and feeding the cows. And you can see from how that boy is, she's a great momma bear, too."

Bella delivered breakfast to them – a plate with a heaping mound of country potatoes beside biscuits and sausage gravy, and a dish of fresh fruit for each. "Can I get you fellas anything else?"

"No ma'am, this looks great!"

Marco joined the men for breakfast and answered a load of questions from Chance about life in the city.

"That place was nice and all, but I don't miss it, except Auntie Angela. She's not really my Auntie, but I call her that. We used to live together. She liked to play with me and take me to the park when Mom was working. And she read the best bedtime stories. I never had a single nightmare when she read to me."

"Sounds like a very special lady." Chance

nodded to his father. "Well Pops, I think I hear a rehab appointment calling my name."

The men took their plates to the kitchen. "Thank you, Miss Bella. That was a wonderful breakfast. We'll see you later."

"You bet. You guys come back anytime." She waved her hand through the air toward the coolers and ovens. "There's always something to eat around here."

She smiled as they left, giving Marco fist-bumps on their way out.

3

___

Rehab wasn't what Chance expected. He thought it would be more like an intense gym workout. Instead he was playing brain games and doing stretch and strength training with his legs.

"But Jackson, there's nothing wrong with my legs."

Jackson was the physical therapist assigned to his case. He was known for his work with injured athletes. He was big, strong, and no-nonsense. If Jackson said to do it, you did it. He looked at his client - a strong-willed man in his late twenties with the eyes of a broken man. Part of Jackson's job was to help his patients recover their confidence and sometimes, like with Chance, redefine who they are in the world. This man should never ride a bull again. Jackson, the doctors, his family—nobody could stop Chance from getting on a bull again, but Jackson admonished him not to.

"I know, Chance. It's early in your recovery and your shoulder needs another month to heal before we can do the hard stuff. I know you're looking forward to all that pain, you adrenaline junkie you."

Chance snorted. He didn't like the pain, but yes, he lived the life of an adrenaline junkie. That's what kept him on the bulls, rising in rank to the top ten in the U.S. in six of the last seven years.

"Well, don't you think until then I could do this stuff at home? These stretches and leg lifts and things?" It bored Chance to be laid up and his mom was driving him two hours every day to get him to therapy. He would rather haul feed to the chickens and lead a horse around. He could get his exercise that way.

"You know that the physical exercises are only part of what we're doing here. You are also getting therapy to work on your memory. That's just as important."

Jackson made some notes on Chance's chart and set his clipboard down. "Listen Chance. Sometimes you don't have control and this is one of those times. I'll tell you what I can do. We have a couple of PTA's that work in the field. Let me do some research and see if there's one in your area who can come over and do therapy at home so you only have to come in here a time or two every week. How's that?"

"Well, I'm not sure what a PTA is. I thought that had something to do with the school moms, but I like the part about not coming in here so often. I like you, Jackson, but I like the ranch better."

"Yeah man, I get that. A PTA is a physical therapy assistant. It's like Rachel who worked with you on Tuesday." Jackson pointed across the room to a bubbly blond twenty-something guiding another patient with a leg brace up and down stairs.

"Dude, I like the way you think! You can send her over and I'll do all my therapies. Promise." Chance smiled at Jackson, his eyes brighter than they had been the entire session.

"Well, Rachel, who by the way is a married woman, doesn't work in the field but there are some others who do. I'll find out what I can and call you later to see if we can make it happen. Deal?" Jackson held his huge hand out to seal the agreement.

Chance grabbed Jackson's hand, gave it a

brief shake then hoisted himself up from the massage table where they had done stretching exercises. "Deal. Thanks."

As THEY DROVE BACK to the ranch, Chance shared the good news with his mom. "The only thing is, Jackson wasn't sure they had anyone on staff in our area. Have you ever heard of someone like that, Mom?"

"Let me think. There is someone…" Yvette knew everyone in Buffalo Ridge where she had lived all her life. It was a small town - one thousand people year-round and in the summer it doubled in size with seasonal workers coming in to work the tourist attractions. The town was perched on the edge of the Badlands, a site that drew a million visitors every year to inhale the beauty and dramatic character of the uniquely carved landscape.

"Yeah, I know. Pauline Whyte. She does that kind of work. She used to work in the city but now she's back in Buffalo Ridge helping to take care of her dad."

"Biggie Whyte? Is that her dad? I'm surprised he's still alive. I thought he drank himself to death years ago." Chance, restrained by the neck brace, watched the road ahead. They passed car after car from states other than South Dakota. "Last time I saw him, he was in a brawl outside the Wild Bison bar on Main Street. As I recall, Joe Grund made some comment about Biggie's wife being a Sioux. Biggie didn't take kindly to whatever he said."

Biggie Whyte was a giant man, a combat vet with a wild temper and insatiable appetite for alcohol. He married Loretta, a sweet Native American woman from the reservation south of the Badlands. She didn't want to live in Buffalo Ridge, but there wasn't enough work for Biggie on the reservation. He was a good ranch hand, when he was sober and showed up for work. The Davies ranch hired him several times over the years.

"Biggie's in a bad way. Not only is his liver shot, but he's got brain cancer too. He's too much for Loretta to handle. She's working three, four jobs all the time to pay the bills. She's such a sweet lady. I really feel for her. She's worked so hard all her life and as mean as Biggie is, she won't leave him."

Yvette turned the flasher on to pass a car. "Don't you just wonder what these folks are thinking, driving fifty miles an hour on the interstate?" She signaled again and pulled back into the slow lane. "Anyway, Pauline came home when the doctors diagnosed Biggie's brain cancer. He went through a time when he got downright mean at home but now, he can barely speak and he no longer walks. Hospice comes in to help the family but Pauline's shouldering the heavy load at home."

"She must have been younger than me in school. I kind of remember her but don't think I've seen her in years." Chance adjusted his immobilized arm and drew a long drink of soda from the bottle.

"She's always been quiet. I think she was probably teased when she was young. It couldn't have been easy in this town to be the daughter of Biggie Whyte and a Native American mom. She's sweet, though, and I know she used to sing some. She has a beautiful voice."

"Even if she doesn't work for the same PT agency, maybe they could contract with her or we could directly. This drive is just a waste mom. I appreciate you taking me, but I know you have better things to do."

"It's been fun getting to spend this time with you, but yes, I get it. How about if I reach out to Pauline and see if she would be willing? Then we can give her name to Jackson and they can talk with her about her preference." Yvette pulled off the interstate to head south to the ranch. "Need anything from town before we head home?"

"You know, I really haven't been downtown. Would you mind if we just went down for a quick stroll?" Chance used to hate town this time of year, when the tourists crowded the sidewalks and took all the parking spots on Main Street.

"I don't mind at all. Loretta's probably working at the soda fountain in the big store. I can get Pauline's number from her. Besides, your old friend Rick Lyle is a manager there. He'd be so happy to see you."

"Wow. I can't believe Rick's still around here. Guess he decided it's a good place to raise that big family of his. I hope they're paying him well as a manager. He's such a hard worker." Chance and Rick spent years racing one another in track, high jumping and playing basketball. In a small school like theirs, they had opportunities to play multiple sports. If they didn't, there would be no team. Rick was from a ranch family but rodeo never got in his blood the way it did for Chance.

Yvette found a place to park. They had to walk three blocks to get to the store; a long-time tourist attraction with free animated cowboy or-chestras, a Jurassic Park dinosaur, and lots of stuff to buy from cheap imported salt and pepper shakers to expensive fine art.

"Well, I'll be. Look who's here folks! My friend Chance Davies, the famous bull rider." Mike greeted Chance in the old dining room. Local ranchers' brands hung on wooden plaques. Huge hand-carved wooden statues of famous Native American chiefs and explorers stood in the enormous rustic room. A hodge-podge of western art covered the massive walls.

Chance reached his friend's hand first and shook it firmly. "Mike, so great to see you. You're looking good."

"I heard about your accident. Tough break, man. How are you doing?"

"I've had better days, but all things considered, I'm not bad. Mom here has been taking great care of me and it's nice getting reacquainted with the ranch. It's fun to see the new livestock and all the stuff Steve's got going on with the dude ranch and stuff." Chance grinned. He waived to a family friend in the background.

"Yeah, that dude ranch is something else. The owner here was at their grand opening and said it was phenomenal, from the entertainment to the food. Reviews from the tourists I've talked to are great. Sure isn't hurting our business any."

"This place just keeps growing, doesn't it?"

Chance noticed the new buildings across the street associated with the store.

"It does. It's nice working for someone with a big vision. Keeps it from being boring, even though it's mostly a seasonal big business. Our winters are still pretty quiet, mostly just locals around here after hunting season, but the summers sure make up for it. Anyway, I better let you go. Hope to see you around again. Think you'd be up for dinner with Erica and I?"

Chance looked down at his boots. Erica Knape was his last high school girlfriend. Their parting was hard. She went to college instead of joining Chance on the circuit. He sulked for months after they split. Halfway through her college, Mike called Chance to tell him that he was dating Erica and asked her to marry him. It was a bitter pill for Chance but he bucked up and congratulated his good friend. Chance returned to Buffalo Ridge for their wedding, right after she graduated from college. He hadn't seen her since. He wondered if she was the same fit, beautiful brunette after having babies.

"That would be nice. I think I will be around for a while. I need more therapy with this thing." He lifted his restrained elbow just enough to draw attention to his wounded wing. "You've got what, five kids now?"

"That's right. The last two, twin boys, surprised us but hey, we're having a lot of fun with them. Erica's taking a couple years off teaching to enjoy them while they're little." Mike beamed when talking about his family. They were his everything. "I'll call you, maybe in a few weeks when it slows down here. Okay?"

"Wonderful. Take care and, it was good to see ya. Tell Erica 'hey' for me." Chance turned to walk out. His mother tucked her arm in his good one as they strolled through the alley to the backyard of the store.

"He is a great guy. He's becoming a pillar in this community, like his folks were. Hey, there's Loretta. Let me get Pauline's number."

"Sure, sure. I will go into the candy store. I've got a hankering for something sweet." Chance had also seen a pretty girl behind the counter. Since he was going to be around, he might as well exercise his social muscles. With all the college kids and locals working in the stores this time of year, he surely could find some pretty filly to hang out with.

4

———

"Okay Chance, squeeze this gel ball."

Chance took the orange ball from Pauline and squeezed it with his good hand. "Like this?"

"Yes, just like that, but with your other hand while repeating back to me the list of words I told you to remember. Ready?" Pauline shook her head, took the ball back and put it in Chance's other hand. With his arm still immobilized, they could work with his hand and wrist to keep strength and range of motion. Three more weeks and they would do the harder exercises that bring grown men to tears. She wasn't looking forward to that and hoped the physical therapy office in the city would do most of that. It hurt her to see her patients in that much pain.

"Refrigerator... magnifying glass... and I think that's really two words, purple... person, find, distance... jacket, round, soldier, quick, symptom, oatmeal...that's it, right?

"That's fantastic Chance, but there are three more. Turnip, wheel, and light bulb. But that's the most you have done so far. High five!" Pauline raised her hand to meet his free hand in the air.

Pauline knew of Chance but didn't really know him. His brother Jesse was closer to her in age and she knew Jesse from school. Chance was famous in their small town though; bull riders who make it big were like NFL quarterbacks around here. If she was anyone else, she might ask him for his autograph. But she didn't care. Survival in daily life consumed her. These few hours a week with Chance were a welcome respite from the difficult work of caring for her dad. Biggie Whyte was a tough man to love. As a child, she looked up to him. He was strong, always had her back and talked about how their family would always be together; nothing could tear them apart.

As she grew older, and his drinking increased, she saw his faults. He sent his wife off to work but he rarely worked himself. He recoiled when his wife showed affection but commanded her to their room for 'adult time' whenever he wanted. He had only one friend that Pauline knew of, and she couldn't understand why Foster was his friend. They weren't drinking buddies, yet Foster bailed her dad out of many bad situations. They fished, sometimes, and sat around and talked about the war. Days long gone, trapped in their memories, kept them from being present in today's life.

"Hey Pauline, can I ask you something?" Chance had been wondering about this girl, the wallflower he looked forward to seeing for therapy. He didn't wait for her response. "Do you think my memory will ever come back all the way?"

Chance sounded sad. Pauline recognized sadness. The softer, monotone voice, eyes downcast, shoulders rounded. She lived it and she hated it. "I think you're making great progress, Chance, and you should be proud of that. I've worked with some patients with head injuries, like from car crashes, and they couldn't do a fraction of what you can. Be proud Chance, and remember, it's at least three months before your brain is healed from the initial trauma. Okay?"

"Thanks, Pauline. I will try." He looked at his helper. She had one of those faces; a face of experience with faint lines drawn across the forehead, dark narrow eyes, but the skin of youth. Pauline was six years younger than Chance, which is why he did not know her in school. She easily shared the basics but didn't talk much about herself.

"You know, I'm really glad you could take me on as a patient. I know with your daddy being so sick that it must be hard to leave him to help me out."

"Oh, no. It's easy. I mean, I have to time it so my mom can be there with him but honestly, I really appreciate the break. And as far as patients go, you're not bad." She smiled at him, her thick lips framing perfect teeth. She was thin and looked almost underfed, but Chance knew that her mother was a tiny woman. Pauline had many of her mother's Sioux features, but there was an exotic element. Her skin was olive, her cheekbones high. Chance thought she was very attractive, not in the fun filly way, more of the moody, shifting light on a cloudy day way.

"So Pauline, tomorrow I can't do therapy. My therapy is going to a birthday party for a five-year-old cowboy. Are you available after the weekend to come out and do more exercises?

"Sure. That sounds fine. I didn't know you had a son."

Chance laughed. "I don't. The boy is the son

of the cook at the dude ranch. It's his special party and there are some extra-special surprises coming his way. He is one lucky little dude."

"Oh, sorry. I just assumed. Well, you have fun at the birthday party and I will see you in two days."

Chance walked Pauline out to her car, an old Bonneville that had seen better days. Pauline waved goodbye through the open window. Chance raised his hand, turned and walked out to the stables.

"Now that's a beautiful Paint, Jesse. I didn't realize you were getting another horse. What are you going to do with this one?" Chance rubbed his hand along the horse's neck and shoulder.

"Nice, huh? This isn't mine. Steve picked it up for Marco."

"Marco? That's some birthday present. Say… what do you think is going on over there at the dude ranch?"

"What do you mean? It's a dude ranch." Jesse pulled his brows together. It seemed an odd question to him.

"I mean with Steve and Bella. She's a looker, and he seems so much… lighter, not so moody as the last time I was home."

"Well, the last time you spent any time with him was not long after Vikki died. He was sad for a long time but he's having fun with the dude ranch. He's a teacher at heart and he gets to lead show and tell with his guests all the time. And Bella, well, Bella is a surprise. We did not know what to expect from a pretty little Italian coming from the big city. And Marco, well, he was the biggest surprise. Nobody knew about him until the day they drove in." Jesse smirked, remembering her arrival.

"Is that right?"

"Yeah. I came up behind her on the gravel road over there by the turnoff to Johnson's. I came up over a hill and had to slam on my brakes to avoid her tail end. Seems her phone map couldn't find the ranch. Anyway, she followed me over there and we were talking in the yard when a little voice comes from the back seat. Freaked me out but Steve was about ready to send her packing."

"Oh yeah! Mr. Control Freak would not have liked that. So, how come she's still here?"

"Well, his back was against the wall. He needed help to open and honestly, it was the best thing he could have done. She has been a real trooper and damn, that girl can cook!"

"So, is it just a boss-employee relationship they have or is something else going on?" Chance wondered if maybe she was available.

He was used to women and girls throwing themselves at him and missed the attention.

"Well, neither one of them have ever said anything to me but I'm a little curious myself. I mean look at this horse, and there's another surprise. He's flying in Bella's best friend from New York for the birthday party. I mean, doesn't that say something?"

"In my world it does, but then I live a different life from you all. Well, I appreciate the heads-up on the surprises. Think I'll go for a walk. Tired of being inside so much."

"Chance, do you think you can clean out a pickup? We need to haul some stuff down to the creek tomorrow for the birthday party. You can drive there, right?"

"Um, sure. I wasn't thinking of going though."

"Oh come on! I think you might enjoy the day out. Why don't you come along?"

"Yeah, okay." Chance spoke hesitantly. "I need to go through my pickup anyway. There is probably some old laundry to throw in the wash. Mom will like that."

Both chuckled as Chance walked away.

The frenzy started early the next day with Yvette bossing everyone around. "Hey Chance, go to the garage and grab three blue lawn chairs.

Put 'em in your truck. We'll want them down at the creek."

Yvette cleared the dishes from the table as she gave orders. "Jesse, before you trailer that horse, will you take these coolers here and pack some ice in one? There's an extra bag in the pantry freezer. Then put them in the truck, too."

The boys obliged their mother. There was no use ignoring her or disputing with her. She had a plan and she would see it through, one way or another. They got the jobs done and soon joined Steve and the rest of the party at the dude ranch.

"Hey Chance, is it all right if Angela rides with you?" Bella's friend Angela had arrived that morning; a long-legged redheaded beauty.

"Sure, that's no problem but there are plenty of horses."

"Sorry, I don't ride." Angela backed away from Marco's surprise horse, Jackalope, and moved toward Chance. "I can tackle a three-hundred pound patient in the emergency room, but horses? They're bigger than that. I'm just not comfortable yet. Think I need some lessons, maybe."

Angela didn't often retreat easily from a challenge, but this morning was just too soon for her.

"Well, we can see that you get lessons, if you

want. It's fine. You can ride with me. I can't be on a horse for at least a couple more months, which is just killing me. I've got room in the pickup for you, and it's fairly clean." Chance winked at Jesse, a silent thank you for the heads-up to clean it out.

Chance and Angela got to the swimming hole where the party would be about thirty minutes before the others. They pulled out the chairs and blankets that Yvette sent along for the day.

"Have you been here before?" Angela had never been to a swimming hole before; her picnics had all been in manicured parks. She struggled to spread the blankets evenly on the thick, untamed grasses.

"Sure. It was a regular thing for us to come down here, first as a family, then alone when we were big enough to drive. Around here, that's about eleven."

"You drove at eleven?" Angela looked up at Chance with eyes wide. "That sounds dangerous."

"Look around. What kind of trouble can we get into out here? It's not like the city where there's an accident waiting to happen every ten feet."

Angela laughed. "Yes, you are so right. So, cowboy, tell me what it's like to be a bull rider."

"Well, I'm guessing it's a little like working in an inner city emergency department. It's like living life eight seconds at a time. That's how long you have to stay on the bull to get in the money. I'm probably a little like you—an adrenaline junkie. Don't you just kick it into high gear when that bad accident happens and your emergency room floods with bloody patients?"

"I think you've seen too many hospitals on TV," Angela smiled. "But yeah, it's a little like that. I couldn't do what Bella does. It seems like the same thing over and over again. What I see and do is different every day."

"Yeah, me too. Every bull has its own personality and its own style. As a rider, it's my job to dominate them. Can you imagine the ego it takes to think two hundred pounds of me can dominate the muscle of a one-ton beast bred solely to throw people off its back?" Chance had thought about this a lot over the years and owned it. He had to have a great deal of confidence in his ability or he shouldn't be stepping a foot in that arena.

"Must make you attractive to the cowgirls then, eh?" Angela flashed a flirty smile at him. He was cute, in a ruggedly handsome, well-built athletic way. Rougher around the edges than her usual attraction but hey, when in Rome…

"Yeah, I've had a buckle bunny or two give me their numbers." Chance winked at her.

"Buckle bunny. That's funny! I never heard that one." Angela leaned back on the blanket, her long legs stretched out for Chance to see.

"Well, we are the rock stars of the rodeo. Honestly though, it's never been about that for me. It's really about self-discipline and making a living. Leaves me wondering what I will do now. I never trained for anything else." Chance looked away, hoping to see the rest of the group coming down the trail.

"You'll figure it out. You'll probably come up with something special. That's what happens, you know. You get backed against the wall and your best ideas come. I've seen it repeatedly."

"Well, I appreciate your confidence. I'm trying not to get too concerned about it."

"You know, when Steve and Bella called me the day of the accident, he walked me through what happened with you and that bull. I just can't imagine what it would be like to have a bull fling you around."

"Yeah, I've seen it happen to a few guys. Knew one who didn't make it. Tell you what; Jesse has the video of the ride. I haven't seen it yet, but he will put it up on the TV tomorrow so we can see it on the big screen. One of our friends who runs a rodeo school wants to come over and take a look at it. There may be something in there he can use in his training. Care to come up to the house and join us?”

“Yes, I want to see that. Hey, look! They’re coming there on that hill.” Angela traced the line of riders across the horizon with her finger, smiling at little Marco, birthday boy, riding his own new pony. He and Bella were so happy. She wondered if she could ever find that happiness on the prairie.

5

"Hey Angela, come on in! Here, have a seat by me—best seat in the house." Chance patted the cushion next to him on the couch where she would have a good view of the big screen TV.

"Angela, this is our friend Paul Scotsman, a great rodeo man."

Paul tipped his hat. "Nice to meet you, ma'am."

"Hi there." Angela looked the man over, a cowboy through-and-through. Pleasant manners, hat, boots, jeans, and a slight stoop from a back that toiled intensely.

"Jesse, are you ready to put this video on?" Chance called out to his brother. "He's the only one who has seen it. He says he couldn't

48

watch the whole thing. It's gruesome, he says. I got to tell ya, the way I felt when I woke up in the hospital, I'm thinking it must be pretty bad."

"Yep. If you're all ready, I'll start the thing." The room fell silent, and they nodded in unison.

The video showed a clean break through the gate. Chance pulled up tight on the rope, spurring and inching his center of gravity to match the bull's moves. Big Brutus hurled his body right, then left, kicking high to free himself of the irritant on his broad back. Chance kept his eye on the spot between his shoulders to stay with the bull as he moved, shifted position to keep up with the brute and hooked his spurs again and again as the bull thrashed about. Dust rose from the arena floor but Chance held tight as the animal kicked to free the flank strap. The buzzer sounded. Eight seconds done. The crowd cheered. Brutus threw Chance into the well, that space at the center of the bull's curled body and he struggled to get his hand out of the rope. The arena fell silent as the bullfighters worked to distract the bull so Chance can free his bound hand.

Angela reached over to Chance and squeezed his thigh. He covered her hand with his free hand and squeezed it gently. She looked up at him, eyes wide with panic as she anticipated what would flash on the screen next.

"Pause for a second." Yvette ran to the door to let Pauline in. She brought her into the family room to join them, explaining what they were watching. "It'll just be a little longer, then he'll be ready for his therapy. Okay, Jesse, you can play again."

The video showed Big Brutus raging against the drag. Chance tried to free his trapped riding hand when the bull swung his head around and flung Chance over his back with his horn. This move allowed Chance to get free, but he quickly lost consciousness and his riding arm hung limp, the shoulder muscles shredded. Big Brutus continued his rampage. He landed a hoof on Chance's shoulder. His show continued as he ran the bull fighters up the fence. Meanwhile, Chance's score of a remarkable ninety-three points flashed on the screen.

The room was silent for about thirty seconds when the video ended.

"Man, I don't know whether to congratulate you on the score or cry for you—the way he tossed you around like a rag doll." Paul had his own scars from years of riding. He understood the passion for the sport, the athleticism it commanded and the tremendous feeling of loss that followed an accident like this.

"Yeah, me neither." Chance swallowed hard. His stomach churned. "That raunchy beast dominated me. That's hard to stomach."

His grip on Angela's hand had tightened during the last part of the video. He sighed, let it go and she put it back in her lap.

"I know what you mean. These things happen. Fortunately for the sport, it doesn't happen often, but like I say, the more times you climb up there, the greater the chance you will have an injury. It's just too bad it had to be you Chance." Paul didn't want to say it, but if this didn't stop Chance's career, he had a different kind of sickness.

The group broke up. Angela went back to the dude ranch to spend time with Bella and Marco. Chance and Pauline did some exercises in the yard, working on his lower body strength and balance.

"Sorry you had to see that. I hadn't seen the video, but now that I have, I have a better understanding of my injuries." Pauline was efficient with her exercises. She didn't spend any time on small talk today like she had recently.

"That's okay. I've seen some cowboys get hung up out at the rodeo grounds. It's scary. But to see it on the big screen with such a brawny bull, it's shocking." Pauline steadied him as he worked on the balance platform she brought out for him to practice on. "It's pretty amazing you're still able to do all this."

They moved on to stretching and strengthening exercises for the hand and wrist of his immobilized arm.

"This thing is really getting to be a nuisance." Chance lifted his elbow inside the straps holding his shoulder down. "Gotta tell ya, I'm itching to get back on a horse."

"Oh, I'm sure. It's only a couple more weeks until you get that thing off and can start rehabbing that shoulder." Pauline guided him through some wrist and hand stretches. "I know you know it but, I have to say it. If you do too much too soon you risk getting hurt and it could be worse for you."

She made some notes and looked up. "We have gotten through today's exercises. Maybe you and Angela can find something fun to do to take your mind off things." She raised her eyebrows, challenging him to do something to ease his restlessness.

"Yeah, she's only here a couple more days. She leaves on Wednesday. I'll take her out tomorrow and show her some sights, if I can pry her away from Bella and Marco." Escorting the lovely Angela around town would be an ego boost. She was a beautiful woman with a cosmopolitan air not seen in these parts. Chance found it refreshing. "Thanks Pauline. I will see Jackson for a reassessment Wednesday then I probably won't see you until the end of the week, right?"

"That's right. You get a little reprieve from my torture." Pauline gathered her things to put in her car.

"To be honest, I like your torture. It's been nice getting to know you. Say, how's your dad doing?"

"Uh, thanks for asking. He's got a new infection. Some days are better than others but he's not cured, that's for sure."

Pauline drove away slowly, in no hurry to get to home, a place filled with heartache, darkness and bitterness. She much preferred the light and love of the ranch and the Davies family, even if it was just a few hours a week.

Chance spent the next couple of days sneaking Angela away when Bella was busy. He showed her several of the tourist attractions in the sixty-mile radius. They rode a steam engine, walked to the base of Mount Rushmore, explored Badlands National Park, visited a bison ranch, explored the ranch and watched the livestock.

"I see why Bella loves it here. It is so free, clean and quiet and the people are all so nice. Nothing but the birds to wake you in the mornings and stars to escort you into slumber at night. But…" Angela craved the busyness of her emergency room, the drama of the hospital like a soap opera, and the sounds of the city.

"It's not like the city, is it? The sirens and car horns are your lullaby, aren't they?" Chance had spent a lot of time in Vegas, Oklahoma City and other cities for big events. He wasn't uncomfortable there; he preferred wide-open spaces.

"That, it certainly is not. But, even the few days I have been here have left me refreshed, and my heart is so full to see my friends so happy. Do you think this dude ranch will be a lasting endeavor for your brother?" In the city Angela stopped naming a favorite restaurant, as they seemed to come and go faster than her patients. Chance shrugged unknowingly.

<hr>

CHANCE AND YVETTE took Angela to the airport since he had an appointment at the rehab center in the city. She promised to return for a visit and invited them to spend time with her in Manhattan. "You are all welcome any time and thank you. Thank you for being a family for Bella and Marco. I can't imagine a better life for them right now."

Physical therapy with Jackson was brutal as he pressed for a wider range of motion. He was pleased to see Chance's progress. "How are things going with Pauline? It seems to me she's helping you keep up your strength."

"Pauline has been great, and she's such a kind girl. Thanks for making the connection for us. I like you and all, but I'm glad we don't have to drive in as often."

"Sure, sure. This is the first time I've worked with Pauline, but she's done an excellent job of providing me updates and asking for guidance as you've progressed. She's a keeper and I'm going to see if she's interested in coming on staff."

"I can highly recommend her if you need a referral." Chance had a soft place in his heart for Pauline. She was more than the wounded doe she initially appeared to be. She had lived through a lot in her young life but her goodness remained intact. She shared none of her drama with Chance, but all of her positive outlook and integrity. He liked that. He liked her.

Chance was restless on the ride back to Buffalo Ridge. His head hurt and he wanted some distraction. "Hey Mom, I think I'll drive into town when we get home and just get out for a bit. I'm feeling restless."

"Sure honey. It must be hard not having the same freedoms you had just a few weeks ago. I'm counting on you to let me know when your father and I are overstepping our boundaries. We know you're an independent cuss and we don't want to keep you from living your life."

Yvette thought she had negotiated that balance well, giving Chance independence while keeping him safe. She knew there would be a day when he would be ready to leave again. Hopefully that wouldn't mean he would return to bull riding.

Downtown Buffalo Ridge was busy. There were tourists galore, but the local regulars and imported summer help still gathered at the local watering holes. Chance wandered into a diner and bar, a place guaranteed to provide entertainment.

"Hey Chance! Man, how you doing?" Justin Keilly had been in Chance's class. He skipped college, despite a great high school performance.

His father fell ill and his mother needed him at the ranch. He, like most guys his age, followed Chance's career closely He held out his hand to Chance. "So sorry to hear about your accident. Glad to see you up and about."

"Hey Justin, good to see you. I'm… um….a bull rider… uh, yeah, I'm good. Thank… you."

Justin, like everyone else, had heard about Chance's serious head injury and being in a coma for several days. People with head injuries, in Justin's experience, sometimes had a hard time tracking conversation. He noticed the limp handshake. It was hard to imagine Chance as anything but the all-star athlete he was in high school, with girls swooning for him.

"Hey Chance, how about joining me for a bite to eat?" Justin hadn't planned on eating, but had a niggle in his stomach preventing him from leaving Chance alone.

"Uh… okay. Can I get a me… mell… uh, melomonaide drink?" Chance reached up to rub his head. He felt like someone wrapped his head in insulation. His hearing was not sharp and his thinking was dull. He looked to Justin, his face pinched with anxiety and uncertainty.

While following the hostess to a booth, Justin caught sight of Pauline Whyte walking by the window of the restaurant's glass door facing

Main Street. "Excuse me just a second Chance. I'll be right back."

Justin rushed out the door and called out to Pauline. "Hey, Pauline!"

Pauline turned around on the busy sidewalk and returned to the entrance of the diner. "Hey, what's up?"

"I heard you were working with Chance Davies."

"That's right. But according to HIPAA, I can't really tell you anything." Pauline valued her PTA license and her work with Chance. She didn't want to jeopardize that opportunity, one that dropped into her lap at a time when she really needed it.

"No, I don't want to know anything. Just think you can help me. I ran into him inside and he doesn't seem right. Can you come talk to him?"

Justin had heard that Chance was doing really well, so it surprised him that Chance couldn't carry on a conversation. Even more concerning was the constant massage of his head, like he was trying to rub away the pain or organize his thoughts.

"Sure, sure. I haven't seen him for a couple of days but he was doing really well when I did see him."

Pauline followed Justin into the diner. When she saw Chance at the table, she knew immediately that something wasn't right. The right side of his face was drooping, and he was leaning to that side.

"Pauling, howsu… doin?" Chance looked at Pauline, his eyes unable to focus, his mouth restricted to moving only on the left side.

"Hey Chance, it's nice to see you." Pauline reached her hands out to Chance. She leaned in, to smell his breath and whispered in his ear. "Have you been drinking Chance?"

He didn't smell like it. He shook his head in the negative. She turned toward Justin and spoke quietly, wanting to avoid any panic. "Justin, call an ambulance."

She looked back toward Chance, recognizing the signs similar to a stroke. "Chance, here, squeeze my hands."

Chance lifted his left hand but his right would not budge. He couldn't make it meet Pauline's hand even though he wanted to. She hoped that Dave from the hardware store had help in the store today. He was the closest EMT from the small town's volunteer ambulance service.

"This will sound a little silly Chance, but can you stick your tongue out at me?" Pauline was increasingly concerned that he had a bleeding vessel in his brain from the original injury.

Chance had difficulty sticking his tongue out, and when it protruded it was not in the center where it should have been. Despite the internal feeling of panic, she spoke calmly. "Hey Chance, we need to have the doctor check you out. I asked Justin to call the ambulance. I'm concerned that there is another bleed in your brain. Don't worry, we've got this."

Chance reached to Pauline. "Sway wit me, puhuleez."

"I will. I'll stay with you until the doctors figure this out. I'll call your mom and let her know we're going to the hospital."

Volunteers from the small town ran the ambulance service. Pauline prayed they would respond soon. She moved into the booth beside Chance, helped him lean back and held his hands. "It's okay, Chance. You'll get through this."

She wasn't sure, but she needed to believe in something.

6

———

Yvette intercepted Pauline as she walked toward ICU room seven, the temporary home of Chance Davies. She dotted the corner of her eyes with a tissue.

"Oh Pauline, dear! Thank you thank you. They say you saved his life. If you hadn't recognized what was going on, he could have had terrible brain damage… or worse."

"So, is he doing better today?" Pauline spoke in a hushed voice, afraid to disrupt the tension hanging in the air like an overfilled balloon. She had followed the ambulance to the hospital last night, and stayed until a few hours earlier. After the hour-long drive home, she bathed her father, changed his bedding and coaxed him into a few sips of a chalky protein drink. When the hospice worker arrived to be with her dad, she anxiously drove back to check on Chance.

"Hey Pauly, is… is dat chu?" Chance called from the room. A smile spread across Pauline's face and she grasped Yvette's wrist. "Amazing… he wasn't even able to coordinate a single sound with his mouth last night. This is great progress, and so early."

Pauline nearly skipped into Chance's room, so relieved and thankful to see him. When he smiled, one side was higher than the other but he was slowly regaining control of his right side.

"So, you weren't drunk, they say." She laughed lightly, then took the first deep breath since she saw him at the diner. She had grown fond of Chance over the past few weeks; more than just an escape from her reality, he was fun and kind to her.

Chance reached out for her hand. "Thas right." He held onto her hand. "So nice ta see you. Sanks Pauly for getting me here."

Pauline let her hand fall into his, hoping he would not let go quickly. She wanted to stay there with him, close, until everything was right in his world. "You're welcome, Chance. It's nice to see you looking so good. You gave me quite a scare."

"You know, I should have put the pieces together yesterday. He told me his head hurt, and he was restless. I just didn…" Yvette dabbed at her eyes again.

Pauline turned and looked kindly at Yvette. "Oh, honey, you couldn't have known. These things happen in our bodies and we can't see them. There would just be no way to know."

Dr. Singleton rushed into the room, his white lab coat covering blue scrubs flying behind him. The only full-time neurosurgeon in this hospital, he had little time to spend on niceties. "Well, young man, you dodged the bullet again. I talked to your doctor in Bellsville and this nice young woman here gave me a rundown of what you've been doing and what happened last night. Son, you've got an angel there beside you. Her quick wit saved you."

Pauline wondered how this man, a tall, muscular African American man with huge hands, could perform delicate surgery in the brain. She knew he was a great surgeon. He treated many of her past patients.

Dr. Singleton towered over Chance, who looked small in that hospital bed with the standard issue nightgown and white sheets. "Son, your brain got beat pretty badly in that accident you had with that bull. It looks like there was an injured vessel that gave way. Fortunately for you, it was a small bleed, and it has stabilized. As you absorb that blood the pressure on your nerves will let up and most, or all, of your function will come back."

"Wilt appen again?" For the first time since she started working with him, Pauline saw fear cross Chance's face. She reached out and stroked his bicep.

"Well, it could but the further out you are from the accident, and the more time that has passes, the less likely it is to happen. For now, we will watch you for a couple more days here in the hospital then I will have them make you an appointment in my office. Until then, you can continue your physical therapy and keep taking life slow. I understand it's got to be hard for someone like you. You're a thrill seeker, aren't you?"

"Yethir, I am."

"I think you might need to redefine what that looks like for you. As someone who knows brains pretty well, I'm strongly suggesting you never ride a bull again. I don't know if that was in your plans, but if you do, it will probably be a death sentence for you." Dr. Singleton looked to Yvette, then Pauline. "These people here don't want to see anything happen to you, and frankly, neither do I."

Chance looked to his mom, then Pauline. He wasn't looking to die, but he surely didn't know who he was without a bull under him and traveling the country with his horses in tow.

"Shanks doc. Got it." Chance felt his eyes brimming. He looked away, not wanting to show weakness in front of the women.

"Okay then, I think we have a plan. I'll be back in tomorrow and the nurses here are great. They'll let me know if anything changes."

Dr. Singleton pushed himself back from the bed rails and nodded to Yvette and Pauline. He rushed out of the room as quickly as he entered it.

"Well, that was fun, eh Chance?" Pauline found a chair in the corner and pulled it up so Yvette could take a seat.

Chance shook his head. "Naw so much."

"Oh, Chancey, you're a fighter. You'll come out of this better than ever. Look at Steve, how he took Vikki's death and turned it into the dude ranch, not to mention all the side projects. You come from strong stock, Chance. And, you've got all of us behind you." Yvette looked to Pauline, nodded, then smiled somewhat weakly to Chance. She looked weary, tired from worry with dark circles under her eyes and hair a bit too long to keep its shape, the grays starting to pop at the scalp.

"Well, hello stranger. It's been what, a week since I saw you last?" Jackson walked into the room. The rehabilitation clinic was part of the hospital. He leaned against Chance's bed and put his hand on his good shoulder. Chance looked at him, his brows pulled together.

"Naw man, I'm kidding you. I saw you yesterday. Pauline left me a message last night to let me know you're here. Thought maybe you'd like to get up and take a walk. They're going to watch you a few days, but that doesn't mean you have to stay flat on your back."

"Great idea. I will take your mom down for coffee and a bite to eat." She turned to Yvette. "I bet you haven't eaten yet today, have you?"

Yvette shook her head as she dug around her purse for her phone. "I'll call your dad and the other kids and give them an update."

Yvette had told the others to stay home until she knew more. There was so much to do with harvest upon them and the dude ranch so busy.

Pauline slipped away to arrange for someone to stay with her dad. The hospice worker needed to leave for another patient before Pauline planned to be home. Several churchwomen had offered to help out. Now was the time to see if they meant it. Ruthie was a retired nurse. She would try her first.

Jackson was sitting Chance up on the side of the bed, testing his balance and wrapping the gait belt around his waist when they left.

"Do you think this will happen to him again, Pauline?" Yvette reached for the elevator button.

"It's so hard to know but I have a gut feeling that it won't. Anyway, I think if he gets a headache like he had yesterday, he'll get in and see someone right away and they can check him out."

They followed the signs through the serpentine halls until they found the coffee bar in the cafeteria.

"Let me get this Pauline. You've done so much already." Yvette reached for her debit card. "What would you like?"

Pauline rarely drank coffee. Her dad used to drink it night and day, his teeth stained yellow and his bad breath, an acrid mixture of stale coffee and decaying teeth. Today, she would join Yvette. "I'll have whatever you're having. I'm just going to go look at their soup and sandwiches. I'll let you know what they have."

They made their choices and sat at a table. Pauline absorbed the activity of the cafeteria. Staff on break traded stories with peers; family members silently prayed for loved ones, unable to taste the food they were stuffing down to keep up their strength. A father brought a young child through, presumably taking a break while visiting a new sibling. Pauline had done a stint in hospital right after her training. It was too depressing for her.

"Sorry, what was that Yvette?" Pauline snapped back to the conversation when she heard 'dating'.

"I asked who you were dating." Yvette repeated. "You're such a pretty girl, and obviously very smart. I just wondered who the lucky guy was."

Pauline looked down and brushed the crumbs off the table. "Oh, I'm not seeing anyone. I've got a full plate, with my dad and all."

Truth was, Pauline had never dated. When she was in high school, Biggie would not allow her to date. When she moved to the city for school and work and lived on her own, she was too busy. Besides, she didn't know who would want to date her. Her Native American features made her stand apart from the usual bleached blonde beauties. The dimples and stunted nose her father gave her looked out of place when she looked in the mirror. In every other way she looked like her Sioux mother.

"Oh honey, that's a shame. You know, Dan and I married nearly forty years ago. I am blessed to have Dan to walk through the tough things and the happy things with. I hope Chance settles down one day too. Not one of my kids is married and I hope they each find happiness with a partner when the time is right."

Pauline narrowed her almond-shaped eyes, a crease folding between her brows. "But Chance has Angela. Don't you think he'll settle down with her one day?"

Yvette laughed. "Angela? Bella's friend? Now what gave you that idea?"

"Well, I saw them holding hands the other day watching the video, and he talks about her… a lot." Pauline was sure she had seen them holding hands and making eyes at each other.

"Oh, no. He just met her. Chance found his match as a flirt with Angela but they are just playing. There's nothing going on there. She's back in New York now. Angela is a nice, interesting and accomplished woman, but she's not meant for our quiet kind of life. Anyway, I hope you find love with marriage, and family, like I did. When you're ready, and if you want it."

"I think you know I didn't have great examples for how to do that. I love my parents, but our house was nothing like yours." Pauline didn't apologize. She held her head high, like her parents taught her to. But deep in her gut she held a hard knot, one that, if she allowed it, would bubble up and overflow, drowning her in sorrow. She tightened the laces that held her together. "Let's go back and see how Chance is doing."

7

———

"Damn it!" Chance threw down the wrench. He was trying to adjust a gate to the corral, and lost his grip repeatedly.

"Hey now. Let's take a break." Pauline sat on the fence walking Chance through the steps of using the wrench. After the latest brain bleed, he had trouble sequencing his actions. "You're just one week out of the hospital and trying to do a two-handed job with a single hand. You shouldn't be so hard on yourself."

Chance walked away. He needed to breathe and get his head together. He was so damn mad that he wasn't the man he used to be. He felt useless around the ranch and too scared to go anywhere else.

After a few minutes, he walked back and picked up the wrench. "Sorry about that. I just… well I need not tell you, I guess."

He looked at Pauline. Her sad eyes caught his attention. "How are you, anyway? And how about your dad?"

"First off, all that frustration you feel, it's related to your head injury. I've seen it happen before."

"Dear god, is this going to be the way I feel for the rest of my life? I can't take that." Chance tapped the wrench against the iron bar of the gate. He wanted to bash the heck out of the gate but reined himself in. That would just create more problems.

"I recall Dr. Singleton saying that your three-month waiting period, to allow your brain to re-absorb the bleeding and any swelling to go down, started over with the new bleed. I'm sorry Chance, but there's no way to know yet just what your challenges will be. But there is one thing I know for certain. You're a fighter and this will not get you down."

Chance reached across the rail and cupped Pauline's bicep in his hand. "Thank you Pauline, really. It means a lot coming from you. You've seen this stuff before and I trust you."

"At least I'm glad you're not calling me Pauly any more." A sparkle returned to her dark eyes as she smiled at him. "Those first few days you couldn't get my name out. I was hoping it wouldn't stick."

Chance playfully poked her ribs with his finger. "Pauly, Pauly, Pauly!"

She laughed. She felt like a teenager flirting with a schoolboy. At least she imagined that's how it would feel.

"You know, Chance, I've been thinking. A change of scenery may do you some good. I heard the Buffalo Ridge high school rodeo is coming up this weekend. I realize it's not the caliber you're used to, but would you like to go?" Pauline needed the change as much as he did. The hospice aide spent more time with her father these days, giving she and her mom a break. His time on earth was rapidly coming to an end. She had mixed feelings about it and nobody to talk to. A distraction seemed the right answer for them both.

"I normally wouldn't be interested, but hey, what do I have to lose?" Chance shrugged his shoulders and kicked the dirt. Life sucked.

"Great. I'll come get you Friday afternoon about three. Until then, you have some exercises to do and I've got something else for you. I'll get it from my car when we walk back to the house." He would not like this, but she had seen it work wonders with others in similar situations.

"What the devil is that?" Chance looked at the leather-bound journal Pauline held out to him. A blank book with lined pages, a charcoal-colored soft cover with a saddle-colored tie to keep peeping eyes out and deep secrets in.

"This is a journal. There is a lot of research now that shows journaling helps to heal. This is your personal therapist. You can tell this book anything you want—the good, the bad, what you had for dinner, how your feet feel in those cowboy boots —whatever. This is just for you. I will not read it but I have one piece of advice. Write as much about neutral or good things as you do the bad things, the things that piss you off or make you sad. Got it?"

"Um, sure, I guess. I've never been much of a writer."

"You've never had a serious head injury before either, so how about you just try it, okay?"

"Yes, doc, if you say so."

"Just try it for four days and then reassess. Twenty minutes for four days in a row. You can do it morning, noon, or night. Whatever feels good to you."

"If you think it'll help this broken cowboy pick up the pieces, then I'll try it 'cause I really don't enjoy feeling the way I do."

Pauline put her hand on his hand holding the journal. "I know you don't and I want to help you. Chance, I know you have a lot to offer and I want to encourage you to find out how you will do that. I hope you agree that getting back on a bull is not an option."

Pauline looked at him for any sign of a response. There it was. That cringe that showed his pain, the pain that started in his gut and seared through him like a hot branding iron, leaving him raw.

"Yeah, I've been thinking a lot about what Doc Singleton said. I might as well go hang myself in the barn, I think. It would be faster than letting a bull drag me around the arena again. I have nightmares about that."

"See, you already have something to write about. Two things, really, the nightmares and Friday's outing." Pauline smiled and turned to get in her car.

"Hey Pauline, thank you. I appreciate all you've done for me."

"You're welcome. I'm counting on you not to back out on our field trip. Got it?" She shouted through her car window as she prepared to leave.

"Got it. See you Friday." Three days with a trip to the city to distract him on one of them. He would make it. He looked forward to getting out of the house.

Yvette was fixing dinner when he got in the house. "Hey Mom. Sure smells good in here."

"Thanks, son. Your dad requested pork chops tonight so I'm fixing some applesauce to go with them. You know, I'm glad we planted those apple trees all those years ago. They've sure been good to us." She fished a cinnamon stick out of the pot of chunky sauce.

"Say Mom, I was wondering. What do you think of Pauline?" Jessie dropped his new journal on the counter and pulled up a stool.

"Well, I find her refreshingly simple." Yvette always was one to call it as she saw it.

"Mom! That's not very nice." Chance shook his head and looked down.

"Oh honey, I guess it didn't sound nice, did it? It really is a compliment, I think. She's smart. I don't mean simple in that way. I mean she isn't high maintenance. She doesn't seem to need fancy jewelry or the latest designer clothes. She's beautiful with no fuss. That's what I meant. I think she's sweet, and she's dedicated to her parents. Those are the important things, I think."

"Yeah, she is all that. I just wonder if she's happy. She doesn't talk much about herself but she sure seems to be able to figure me out. She gave me this journal. Says it's backed by science and I should write in it." Chance trusted Pauline so he would try it.

Yvette paused, salt shaker midair. "You know, I've heard of that. I think it's a good idea, for whatever that's worth."

She returned to her work. Chance kept his mother company while she prepared dinner. She was a great cook and seemed to be able to make a feast out of very little. There were times, when he was much younger, that beyond the meat in the freezer and the eggs coming every day, they didn't have much in the pantry. The bounty of the garden had been devoured quickly, and they may not have even planted the new garden, and if they had, it may not have produced much yet. Three strapping boys and a tomboy sister could eat a ton.

After dinner he went to his room. The journal lay on his desk. He sighed and sat in front of it. "Do I really want to do this?" he thought. "I might open a can of worms."

He knew the rage he carried these days, the

fear, the sorrow. On some level he knew it; he just didn't know what to do with it. He unwound the leather strap and lifted the soft leather. Leather — that reminded him of the chaps hanging in the tack room. How many miles had they traveled together? On the first page, in feathery writing, Pauline left a message. *Frost the cake, take out the garbage, scream at the trees, and ride the bull, if you must. In these pages, you can go anywhere and do anything you want. Heal, cowboy, heal. Pauline.*

Chance smiled and shook his head. There was something special about Pauline. A touch of creativity, brains, looks and ambition all served up messy. She had a lot going on in that head of hers. And so did he.

That night, Chance baked a cake. He had seen his mother do it a hundred times, likely more. His cake was special. In his cake he threw three handfuls of sand, two of water from the creek, nasturtiums from the front garden, oil from the old grease can in the implement shed and he baked it in an old coffee can on the barbecue. He made a joke of it, something that came naturally to him. He knew eventually he would have to get serious and dig deep but he wasn't ready. He had to stew longer.

On Friday at three, Pauline drove into the

yard to pick Chance up. "Hey cowboy, look at you!"

Chance had shaved and got a haircut. The baby blue plaid western-cut shirt looked great against his dark skin. His sad blue eyes came to life. He was hot.

"Yeah, you like?" Chance turned around so she could get a 360-degree view. He smiled and tipped his black Stetson, apparently his dress-up hat. "You look nice too."

Pauline blushed. The cheek bronzer high-lighted her prominent high cheekbones. Mascara darkened her already dark moody eyes. The red choker made her neck look long and delicate, like her mother's.

"Good looking hat you have there." Pauline reached up and ran her hand across the brim.

"Thanks. I figured it was doing me no good sitting in the box, so yeah, here we go." He paused awkwardly for a moment. "Ah… Pauline, and I mean no offense with this, but would you be okay riding in my ride? It just seems a bit more fitting to be in a pickup to go to a rodeo."

"Oh, now you hurt my feelings! You don't think my ole Bessie is big enough?" She stuck her plump lower lip out in a feigned pout.

They both laughed. "Well, it's kinda that I would like to be the one to drive too, and I don't think your little… Bessie… is made for my long legs."

"Fair enough. Nobody has driven me anywhere since… well, probably never. Let's do this."

Pauline settled easily into the pickup seat for the short drive to town. It almost felt like a date.

8

"Hey there, Chance! Good to see ya, man." Old Tom Martin greeted Chance with an enthusiastic handshake. He tipped his hat to Pauline. "Miss."

"How have you been Tom? Good to see you too." Tom was Chance's first bull riding coach. In the first couple of years riding, Tom hauled Chance all over the five-state area so he could get experience in the low profile rodeos. He was like a second dad to Chance, and taught him a lot about living on a low budget, keeping life un-complicated, and following his passion.

"Oh heck, I'm good as the day I was born." Tom was about Chance's height but he no longer stood upright. His forward lean took him two inches closer to the ground and seemed to round out his middle. He pushed his hat back on his head so it didn't obstruct his view with his head hanging low. "Just out here helping a couple young cowboys with their form. You remember them days, don't ya?"

Tom paused and looked Chance over. With one arm still cinched down, he looked to Tom like a real bull rider who had met his match in the arena. "Say, how about you? I heard all about your tough spill up there in Allentown. Tough break, cowboy."

Tom looked from Chance to Pauline, trying to place her, silently flipping through the files of his memory bank.

"I s'pose you'll want me to teach you how I coach now, won't ya." Tom snickered. He had the longest coaching history in the area. Cowboys across the country knew him as a coach who taught excellent foundational skills to youngsters. He was no nonsense and didn't fancy teaching the teenagers or young men. They had too much attitude for Tom. "Ya know I'm real proud of you, son. You really had an outstanding string of rides over the years. Sorry it came to an end for ya, but I always told you to prepare for that day 'cause you never knew when it would come."

Chance cringed at those words. Not the

proud part, the end part. "That's right, you did and, I listened. I'm in good shape, for the shape I'm in."

Chance looked down as he tucked the toe of his boot under a rock and flipped it. "I'm sorry, Tom. This is my friend Pauline. She's helping me do some rehab. Been a real angel to come out to the folk's place and kick my butt some."

"Kinda easy to wallow some, ain't it? Well honey, Pauline, is it?" Tom stretched his hand out. "It's a pleasure to meet you. You look familiar."

He drew his hand back and rubbed his chin. "Hey, ain't you ol' Biggy Whyte's little girl?"

"Yes sir, I am. Pleasure to meet you." Pauline knew this man − an old bachelor living on the north edge of town running a small ranch. She never heard much about him around town, good or bad, but suspected her dad may have done some work for him at some point. Pauline knew her father's work history, and it wasn't good. He'd last a day or two on a job, ask for cash payment, and never come back.

"Say, I sure was sorry to hear about your dad's cancer. I hear he's hanging in there strong though and he's got you and Loretta to thank for keeping him here on earth. Imagine he'll meet his maker one day though." Tom trailed off, thinking about his own health. Being the private man he was, nobody but he and his doctor knew how bad things were inside that broken body of his. By his count, he had three months left on the death sentence the doctor issued last winter. Just enough time to wrap things up at the ranch, get the crops and cattle sold and dish out his belongings.

"He's strong-willed, for sure, but honestly, he's really sick. I don't expect him to be around for the first snowfall." Pauline had made peace with the fact that her dad would pass, or at least she thought she had.

"Well, let him know ol' Tom Martin wishes him the best, will ya?" Tom plunged his hands into his jeans pockets. He was buying his jeans bigger these days, making room for the swelling in his belly from the toxins his kidneys, filled with cancer like other parts down there, could no longer process.

"Well, Tom, really good to see ya out here with another class of boys. We will watch 'em now and see if you're still as good as you were when you helped me out." Chance patted his old mentor on the back. His hand met with a softer man, more frail than Chance remembered. He wondered how his old friend was really doing under all that armor.

As they parted ways, Tom called over his shoulder. "Say Chance, could you come out to the ranch and see me one day this week? I'd like to chat with you some more."

"Sure. You still have your landline in the house? I'll call you and we'll pick a time. That sound okay?"

"Yeah, yeah. That'll work." Tom pulled his chin up and nodded his head. "You kids have fun now, ya hear?"

Chance watched him walk away, a slower, shuffling man than the one that helped Chance pack gear in days gone by. He put his hand on Pauline's shoulder blade and guided her to the spectator stands at the arena.

"They've sure made some changes around here." Chance pointed out the new concessions stand and the cover over the bleachers.

"The city council tries to keep up with the times and supporting rodeo, as a sport for our local kids, is important to them." Pauline read the local newspaper on Wednesdays when it came to the house. It was one of her few sources of information on local happenings, since she rarely went out socially.

"I'm glad to see it, honestly. It's a thriving sport and these kids should all get the same opportunity I had."

They watched the team ropers and saddle bronc riders. As the arena was preparing for the bull riding, Chance felt restless. "Can I get you something from the concessions? I wonder if they still make those steam burgers? I always looked forward to them when I rode out here."

"That sounds good. Let me go with you and see what they have." Chance stood and reached his hand out to help Pauline climb down the bleachers.

The bull riding competition started before they got to the concessions. They hung out on the far end of the arena, opposite the chutes, watching the riders do their best to hang on for eight seconds. Pauline noticed the way Chance gripped the iron fence with his free hand, his knuckles white and forearm tense.

"You okay watching this, Chance?"

"Yeah sure." His voice sounded surer than he felt.

After the first six riders, Chance was shifting from left to right and had backed off the fence a bit. He looked to Pauline and a smile crossed his face. "I was wondering if you'd like to go into town and grab a bite to eat there."

Pauline's eyes lit. Her dimples showed as a wide smile crossed her face. "That sounds great!"

With his free arm around her shoulder, Chance escorted her to the field by the arena where the pickup was parked. He opened the door for her and closed it as she put her seatbelt on. "Now this is a first," she noted silently. "I've never had a guy open a door for me… ever!"

"So, would you like to go to the diner or the steakhouse?" Those were Chance's preferred places to go when he wanted a decent meal. The other places had burgers or pizza, but he was in the mood for steak.

"Let's see. The last time I saw you at the diner you weren't doing so well. I vote for the Wagon Wheel." She liked their broasted chicken, but it had been so long since she was there she wasn't even sure they had it.

"The Wagon Wheel it is. I hope they still have that sirloin they used to have. I'm hankering for a nice juicy steak." It was a short distance to the restaurant. They were both quiet on the drive. Pauline noticed a funny feeling low in her abdomen – a mixture of anxiety and excitement bubbling in there.

"Oh, I didn't think it would be so busy. We might have to wait to get in. Are you okay with that?" Chance found a parking spot down the block. Chance wanted to get her door, it was something his mother and father had taught him and he enjoyed doing it; but that was a new concept for Pauline. They both got out of the pickup at the same time.

They sat at the bar, silver dollars imbedded in its top and brass foot rests lining the bottom, waiting for a table to open in the dining room. Chance smiled and nodded at Alice, a long-time server at the Wagon Wheel. "This place hasn't changed much. It's probably been six, eight years since I was here. Heck, even some waitresses are the same."

"Well, you are in Buffalo Ridge. There aren't too many options for year-round employment here so those who need it keep it when they get it. Alice there is a friend of my mother's. She's helped me a bit with my dad before hospice was more involved." Pauline smiled at Alice.

"Davies, table for two. Davies." The hostess seated them in the packed restaurant. Some locals recognized Chance and greeted him as the two walked by.

"Well, I'll be. Chance Davies. You back to visit the folks? Hey there, Pauline." Mayor Lyle was dining out with his family.

"Hey Marty… and family. Yeah, I'm back healing up this shoulder here. Got a bump on my head that needed some tending to, as well. Pauline here is providing my therapy."

"It's sure good to see you. Let's get together and catch up sometime." Marty looked to Pauline and Chance for their agreement.

"Sounds good. I'll get your number from Mom and call you." Chance planned to see what Marty could tell him about development in the area. What could it hurt to spend some time with an old classmate?

"Good to see you Marty…and Heather." Pauline felt awkward. She wondered if the couple questioned why, if she was there for Chance's therapy, she was out having dinner with him.

When seated, the waitress took their drink orders. The doctors had restricted Chance from drinking alcohol for now. Pauline didn't drink often, but on occasions like this, when she was around many people, it helped. She would have enjoyed a cold beer but didn't want to offend Chance so she ordered iced tea.

"It won't bother me if you want a drink. Heck, I don't even know if you drink, but if you do, go ahead."

"Thanks Chance but no. I'm fine with tea tonight. Besides, I'm here as your therapist. It wouldn't look good if I was drinking." Pauline wanted him to know how awkward it was for her.

"Oh, sorry about that. What I meant was that we became acquainted through my treatment. Not that you were here tonight providing me therapy." Chance blushed. He wanted to smooth his faux pas over but didn't know how. "Should I go back to Marty and clarify?"

"Of course not. I know I suggested you get away from the grind of our usual therapy for a change of pace, but I guess I hadn't really thought of this as therapy."

"No me neither." Chance folded his menu and laid it on the table.

"What do you think we should call this?" Pauline waved her finger, pointing to each of them.

"Well, Pauline, if we have to call it anything, I think we are two new friends going out to dinner, getting to know one another. Now, can we drop the labeling and just get on with dinner?"

Pauline felt scolded. She hadn't wanted to start an argument but sincerely sought clarification. "Absolutely. Can we talk about the rodeo? I want to know what you thought about the saddle bronc and bull riders. Did you see any promise there?"

Chance looked up and smiled. "Now you're talking my language."

He relaxed and for the next ten minutes

talked non-stop about the sport that he loved. He saw some riders that impressed him. They ordered and ate and swapped stories. Both felt much more relaxed by the end of the meal.

"So, who would like dessert?" The waitress recited the half-dozen types of pie they had. Neither of them had room to eat another bite.

"Maybe next time." He locked eyes with Pauline. "What do you say, Pauline?"

"Yes, maybe next time."

9

Chance felt a compulsion to kiss her before she left but stifled it. As messed up as his brain was, he was afraid what he felt wasn't real. After seeing Pauline back to her car, he wrote in his journal. *She makes me nervous, this mysterious woman with the beautiful smile. The pages of her book unfold slowly and I want to read fast. Maybe I need to tell her how I really feel, if only I could be sure what that was.*

When he saw Pauline again after the weekend, she was all business. She bossed him around, with clipboard in hand. She wasn't mean but she seemed distant and professional. "Hey Pauline, can we talk?"

"Sure. What's up?"

"Well, I wanted to thank you for suggesting I

get out and do something. I enjoyed going to the rodeo Friday and dinner was great, too." Chance wasn't sure what to expect from her. He looked past her as he talked, his thoughts somewhere off in the distance. "I hope it wasn't too boring for you."

"Oh, no, it wasn't boring. I enjoyed it, too. It was good for me to be out of the house. I'm glad you enjoyed getting out." Pauline handed him a clear acrylic box. Inside the clear box there were colored boxes of various shapes and sizes. "Let's go over there, to the picnic table. I want you to dump out the pieces and put them back in the box."

Chance looked at Pauline in disbelief. He wasn't a five-year-old learning to put a puzzle together. He was a grown man who needed to figure out how to make a living with his broken brain. He shoved the box back toward Pauline. He spoke with his voice raised. "Can't do it today. I just don't see how that will get me back to work or the life I want."

Pauline recoiled at the sound of his tense voice and the forcefulness of his words. All her life she had heard that tone. Angry words spoken harshly by an angry man. Clenching his jaw and spitting his words, her father gave tongue-lashings that brought far more pain to her heart than a beating would have. Later in life, after the Veterans Administration finally gave him a full evaluation, the doctors diagnosed him with PTSD. Through her work, Pauline discovered the symptoms of PTSD could be like those of a brain injury. It changed the way she reacted to her father, sometimes. The trauma of all those years, when she didn't understand, triggered her reaction. After years of wishing her father would shut up, these days she longed to hear his voice.

"Okay. I get it Chance. You want to be on the other side of this mountain in front of you. If only you could spread your wings and fly over it, I would cheer you on. But unfortunately, it will not work that way. The good news is your arm should come out of that sling tomorrow when you see your surgeon, and then therapy on that can start. It'll be hard, I mean really hard at first. It won't, though, change the wiring in your brain and what we're trying to rebuild with puzzles like this." She held up the puzzle box.

"I am looking forward to tomorrow, to be honest. I know it will hurt but in case you can't tell, I'm not scared of pain."

Chance paused and looked at Pauline. He wasn't upset with her, he knew he wasn't, but she was his audience in that moment. He had shared the same frustrations with Yvette. She encouraged him to get out and help his dad. He tried, but he could only do half of any job. He needed both hands and a clearer head to get things done. He even tried to help at the dude ranch but he couldn't help with the trail rides, the tack, the roping demonstrations. The most he could do was a special appearance where he showed some pictures and talked about the rodeo scene and bull riding.

"I just have to see progress. I feel so useless." Chance felt the tension rise in his shoulders and into his head.

"Today's therapy is over. But before I leave, let's talk about some things you can do, so you can let off some of that rage I can see in you, and find some enjoyment in life." Pauline turned to put things back in the car.

"Rage? This isn't rage I'm feeling. It's frustration. I'm just frustrated that I can't help around here more." Chance lowered his voice, the muscles of his square jaw bulging. He had seen rage in buddies who had tough concussions. That wasn't him. He would never be like that.

"Or is that my broken brain lying to me again?" he thought.

"You know, Pauline, I've got this. You can go for today. I'm going to Steve's greenhouse to help Mom." He couldn't have this conversation.

He wanted his life back and in that life, he didn't need anyone helping him. "I told Old Tom I would visit him, too. You remember; he wanted me to come by."

"Okay Chance. I'll see you in a few days and by then Jackson will have given me the new treatment plan for your shoulder." Pauline opened the squeaky door of her old car.

"We can put some oil on that hinge when you come back. Remind me." Chance had thought of it before but dang it, it just kept flying from his head.

"Will do. Take care."

Pauline raced away, wanting to leave the tension, mixed messages and defeat behind. She needed a reprieve from the intensity of this work with Chance. It was so much easier when they could focus on those things he could measure and see progress in; the amount of weight he could lift or miles he could walk, the clothing he could independently don and doff. It was hard for him to measure and see changes in his speech, cognitive processing and interpersonal communications. For the first time in a very long time, Pauline looked forward to going home.

Chance skipped the greenhouse and went right to Old Tom's place. Tom knew what he was going through; he'd been there himself a time or two. Probably not quite as broken but broken anyway.

Tom was passing through the yard from the house to the barn when Chance drove in. Tom's place wasn't huge, but it served him well. The little three-bedroom house was in good shape when Chance had last visited, three or four years ago. Now it needed a coat of paint and the trees were overgrown.

"Hey Chance, thanks for coming out. Say, I've got to put a couple of things away out in the barn and I could use an extra hand. You've got one of those, right? Could ya help?"

"Of course. What are we working on?"

"I fixed a hydraulic pump on the Massey. I need to lift the cover back into place."

Tom seemed winded by the time they got inside the barn. "Now if you can just lift that end, and I'll take this one and we can put it in place."

Chance could have easily done this job if he had both hands. He nearly could do it alone with just the one. In days past, Tom could have easily done it alone. Age must be catching up with him.

"That's perfect. Thanks, son. Some days I

just don't have the strength I used to." Chance looked around the barn. Several unfinished projects cluttered the workbench and floor. It wasn't the usual tidy place Chance knew from his youth.

"Anything else I can help you with while I'm here? I'm struggling these days to stay busy with this bum shoulder."

"Well not today, but sure, I've got lots of little projects piling up. How about we go sit awhile in the house? I've got some coffee on. You still drink coffee?" Tom motioned through the open barn door toward the house.

"I do. Here, do you want these doors closed?" Chance motioned to the sliding barn doors.

"No, that's okay. I'll be out again later." Tom walked his stooped walk to the house.

"Nice looking horse you have over there. You going to train him?" Chance thought he looked like a blanket appaloosa.

"You remember Donny Walker, up there on the old Lynch place? That's his boy's horse. He wants to learn some roping and Donny wanted me to test him on flexing and loping circles and such and experience the rope a bit. I'll see what I can do, but honestly, my breaking days are long gone."

Chance followed Tom into the house. "Have a seat there, here let me just move them papers."

Tom picked up a pile of papers from the sofa and moved them to his desk, but not before Chance could see that some were medical bills.

"You want anything in your coffee?" Tom called out through the doorway to the kitchen.

"No, I like mine black as night."

Tom returned shortly with two cups of coffee.

He spoke into the coffee cup held in his hands. "Son, I'm not going to beat around the bush none. I'm pretty sick. In fact, the doc says I have only about three more months on this here earth."

Chance froze. The blood drained from his face and when he started breathing again, his breath came out in a windy sigh. "I didn't see that coming Tom. I'm so sorry. What can I do for you?"

"Actually, I think I can do something for you. I can't teach the rodeo school anymore. I would gladly turn my business over to you if you're interested. I've been doing the three-day schools and private lessons, but I got to thinking the other day after I saw you. You and your brother with the dude ranch could both make out if you partner up and hold longer camps. Heck, some of these guys is even holding month long camps." Tom paused to catch his breath.

"Can we just back up a little, Tom? So what's wrong with you and did you get a second opinion?"

"Second, third, it don't matter. They all say the same thing. I had prostate cancer some ten years ago. Had the surgery, but the damn villain came back to life. Got it now in my bones and bladder and kidneys. I told them no more whittlin' away on my old body. Damn, I'm near eighty years old now. I've lived a long, hard life, and it's time to set the plow down." Tom looked into his empty cup. "Say, can I get you a refill there?"

Chance barely touched his coffee. His stomach had suddenly soured, like milk when Mom added vinegar to make buttermilk pancakes. "No, thanks, I'm good here."

Tom returned with a fresh cup of coffee for himself and handed a fig bar to Chance. "Join me in a little snack, will ya?"

"Say, tell me about that Pauline you were with at the rodeo. She's a pretty little girl. Biggie did good there, even if he was a nasty ol' buzzard."

"Yeah, she is pretty, and really smart. Honestly, between us old friends here, I like her a lot, and not just as my therapist, either. But with this messed up head I got, I can't imagine any good-looking filly would be interested in me."

"Son, you're not so messed up. Look, you're driving, walking, talking. You helped me out in the barn. You will be okay. Put your pity party away and start planning yourself a life. You ain't getting no younger. What are you, 'bout thirty now?"

"Yeah, about that."

"Heck, you should be thinking about finding you a permanent place to live and start a family boy."

"Well, that kind of thinking doesn't come easy to me, even when my head isn't broken, but I suppose you're right."

"You know dang well I am. There was many of them years I thought of you as my own son. You spendin' all that time on the road with me and out here on the place. Don't know if I ever told you but I'm an orphan. I was raised by the sisters over there in St. Joseph's in Minneapolis. Landed out here workin' on the railroad." Tom paused again to catch his breath.

"No, I don't think you ever told me the or-phanage part."

"Yeah, I probly never talked much 'bout it. People get all kinda sad when you say you're an orphan. Anyway, that's a long time ago and we're talking about today. I ain't got no kin. Had a wife in my early days but she died and we never had any kids. This place I got here ain't much, but I scratched a living outta it." Tom took a kerchief from his back pockets and wiped his nose.

"I was wondering if you thought you might want to try, too."

"What are you saying Tom? Are you asking if I want to buy your place?" Chance was getting lost in Tom's abstracts.

"No son. I'm asking if I give you this place if you'd take it on. See, if I don't give it to some-one, the county or the state or someone's gonna come here and take it over. Who knows what would become of it then. Heck, they could try setting another one of those big dinosaurs they got up by the service station out here. Buncha tourists running around out here. I can't have that."

"Tom, there's no way I can accept such a gift but I would think about paying you, at least a sizeable down payment on it. I got to tell you, though. I see the surgeon tomorrow about this shoulder. I need to see how much good it will be for me when they test it all out."

"I think I've got a little time left in me. How

'bout this. How 'bout we talk in one week and I'll have my lawyer come on out. One way or another he's going to have to write up some papers."

"Tom, I'll be back in a week with some answers, maybe some questions, and I darn well expect you'll be here to meet with me."

"That's right, son. I'll be right here waiting on ya."

10

"Hi Pauline. This is Jackson. How are you today?"

"Good Jackson. How did your visit with Chance go this morning?" Pauline had the date marked on her calendar, the appointment with the surgeon and follow-up with Jackson for a new treatment plan for his shoulder.

"Not bad, all things considered. He didn't seem quite as excited to have his arm free as I thought he would be. We did an assessment. His range of motion is actually better than I expected this early after surgery and without therapy for that shoulder, but Chance wasn't nearly as thrilled as I was about it."

In Jackson's years of experience, many patients with the type of injury and repair that

Chance had ended up with a frozen shoulder or extremely limited mobility. For Chance, that would have been a devastating blow. Jackson struggled to understand the lack of enthusiasm from Chance and feared it would hinder his ongoing recovery.

"What was his pain level like?" Pauline considered that pain might have overridden his emotions.

"Well, he said it was six out of ten, at the worst. He refused any pain medication. Says he's seen too many cowboys with bad backs hooked on pain pills and he didn't want to be one of them." Jackson wasn't sure that he himself could make the same decision if faced with the same situation. He would have to watch closely to see if the pain interfered with treatment and kept Chance from stretching and moving to the greatest extent possible.

"That sounds like Chance. He's stoic." Pauline had heard him complain, but less about pain and more about his restrictions. He was motivated to work through it and get his complete independence back—with no more doctor appointments, therapies or his mother helping him straighten his shirt when he couldn't reach.

"Right. Well, I did a mini cognitive status exam too. He seems to be making great progress with his memory and higher functioning process-ing." Pauline sent regular updates of Chance's progress, but to see it for himself impressed him. She was proving to be an excellent PTA.

"You're right. He's been managing a check-book ledger for his debit card. At first he protested and wanted to show me how he just looked it up online, but when he couldn't re-member his bank password or how to navigate the website, he agreed. He's gone from figuring out the column headings to doing all the calcula-tions himself. I think having his second hand back will give him a big boost. He will be able to help a lot more around the ranch." The physical assessment findings of Chance's shoulder re-lieved Pauline.

"My biggest concern is that he seems on edge. It may be just frustration or it may be part of his brain injury; we must watch and see. This is a critical time for him to stay in therapy and get back all the strength and mobility he can out of that shoulder. You know this. He could easily get frustrated and stop therapy."

"I understand. He has been irritable with me. He means nothing by it. If it persists after a week or so then I think we have to consider an-other visit with the neurologist, for another opin-ion." In a strange way, Pauline felt validated by hearing that Jackson, too, saw the irritability in Chance. At least it wasn't her being overly sensitive.

"Agreed. Pauline, I can tell you've done a great job working with him and his mother, especially, is very complimentary of all you have done for him. She told me some of the creative things you've done to get him engaged."

"Yvette is such a lovely woman. Thank you for sharing that, Jackson."

"Pauline, I know you're tied up with your dad. How's he doing?"

"It's not good. He's failing more every day but his heart stays strong. It's hard to watch but we're hanging in there and the hospice team has been very helpful. I'm so glad they have been able to build up that team to service our area this past year. Before, we would have had to take him to the city for inpatient care. My mom would never have been able to see him. If she doesn't work, they don't have a place to live." Pauline stopped herself. She did not know why she was sharing these things with Jackson. Her father would have considered this a serious breach of the family rule to keep family issues to family only.

"Well, when things change and you're at a point where you want to work full time, I would love to have you join the team. Honestly, there's so much work in the thirty-mile radius of where you live that we could easily keep you busy and then patients wouldn't have to drive in as often."

"Thanks Jackson. I appreciate that. I will keep it in mind as things change." The two discussed Chance's treatment plan. They would add resistance exercises to the range of motion and flexibility routine. Chance was younger than many of their patients. It was rewarding to work with someone as strong as him and see him regain pre-injury abilities.

"He's planning to see you tomorrow. I hope that still works with your schedule. Watch him, will you, to be sure he doesn't start doing stupid things and reinjure himself, okay?"

"Absolutely. Another setback would be awful for him. I'll keep you posted. Thanks Jackson."

With the call finished, Pauline went back into her parents' house. She had taken the call in her car to prevent others from overhearing any patient information.

Pauline's dad was yellow with jaundice. His eyes were sunken in his thin face. He was wasting away before their eyes but he wouldn't give up. His eyes were rarely open these days, and he didn't speak. He would still take small sips of broth or protein drink when they fed him. That bit of food, and his strong will, were keeping him alive.

Pauline and her mother were dying a little more each day. The weight of caring for a terminally ill loved one, day in and day out, took its toll in ways others didn't understand. The suffering seemed meaningless.

PAULINE GRABBED the resistance bands from her supplies to take to the appointment with Chance. Sitting with her father all night was tiring, but she was excited to start this new chapter with Chance. She hoped he was in a better mood.

"Good afternoon, Yvette." Pauline walked toward the house. Yvette was sitting outside, drinking her coffee.

"Good afternoon honey. How are you today?" Yvette rose without waiting for a response. "Let me grab you a cup of coffee."

She disappeared through the screen door and returned seconds later with a fresh cup of coffee for Pauline.

"Thank you." Pauline held the warm cup between her palms. Some late afternoons were chilly as they moved toward fall. She still preferred to do her work with Chance outside, where he was most at home.

Yvette sat back down and motioned for Pauline to join her.

"I heard the visit to the doctor and PT was a success yesterday." Pauline was eager to hear Yvette's opinion.

"Well, if you mean he got cleared from the surgeon and all the news was good about the condition of his shoulder, then yes." Yvette paused, looking out over the Badlands, the beautiful landscape visible from the deck. "But Jackson pulled me aside and asked some questions about Chance's mood."

Pauline looked around nervously, wondering if Chance could hear them.

"Don't worry, honey. I had him go with his dad to move some equipment this afternoon. I needed the break. He'll be back soon enough. Anyway, I got to thinking. You know, living with him I probably wasn't seeing it, or just learned to tolerate it, but he has been moody since the last time he was in the hospital. I'm concerned that maybe it's not pain, and it's not frustration with his circumstances but he's going to be like that from his brain injury."

"Well, it's still too soon to tell that, Yvette, but it's possible. I have to say, and this may not be worth much, but in my gut I don't feel like it's related to his brain. He has regained all of his abilities now over the past few weeks. Jackson and I did talk about it yesterday and we agreed to keep watching. If it doesn't improve, we will ask for the neurologist to see him. Sometimes it can be depression that happens just from the situation, you know, being laid up and having to change his life so much.

"Oh, sure, I hadn't thought about that. Well, I'm sure glad you professionals are on top of this. A mother doesn't always know best when it comes to this stuff."

"What you see and feel is very important to us, Yvette. I know it's sometimes easy to get blinded when you're in the middle of it but it's still important that you give us your feedback when things come up. Okay?" Pauline reached out to hold Yvette's wrist. She looked into Yvette's eyes, filled with worry and brimming with silent tears.

"What are you doing to take care of yourself, Yvette?"

"Funny you should ask. Bella and I were just talking about needing some girl pampering. We're going in to the spa for manicures, pedicures, and a facial on Friday afternoon. We were wondering if you would like to join us? We know things are not very pleasant in your world these days and frankly, we could all use the pick-me-up."

"That's very kind of you to invite me. I will check in with Mom and make sure everything's covered for Dad. If so, yes. I've never done that before. It sounds like it could be fun."

"Say, do you think there's any way Loretta would come with us? I bet she's never had the opportunity either, has she?" Yvette always liked Loretta. She had her come out and helped Yvette a few times over the years with organizing and deep cleaning. Loretta was tiny, but she was a real hard worker.

"Now that would be a stretch. It's hard for her to leave Daddy even to go to work, but I will ask her."

"Encourage her, will you? You know, he could just as easily pass when she's away at work as when she's sitting by his bed watching him. I know it's hard. I had both my parents living with me in their last years. I understand. But I also know that if we don't take care of ourselves, nobody else will."

Yvette's wisdom didn't fall on deaf ears. Pauline did not get this kind of guidance and attention from her mother. Loretta lived with no excess and never complained.

Chance drove in the yard. He was slow to get out of the pickup and when he did his face and neck were tense.

"Hey Pauline. I'm sorry you drove all the way out here." He rubbed the upper part of his arm near his shoulder. "I'm not going to be able to do anything today."

"Chance Davies, what did you do?" Yvette stood up to confront her son as he walked up the porch stairs.

"I found a gate down over on the old Webb place and strung it back up."

"Oh Chance. I can't believe you!"

"Mom, don't start in on me now." Chance stormed into the house. His shoulder throbbed. That was all the scolding he needed.

Yvette looked at Pauline. "Here we go. Two steps forward and one step back. He will screw that shoulder up and be in worse shape."

Pauline swallowed the last of her coffee and sat back in her chair, thinking of the best way to approach this, an inevitable situation. She decided she would try to talk to Chance, not about doing too much, too soon, but about immediate pain relief with hot and cold packs.

"Yvette, have you got a heating pad and an ice pack? I'm going to give this a try. If he comes at me with a shotgun, call Sheriff Kennedy, will ya?"

"If he comes at you with a shotgun, I'll do a heck of a lot more than call the sheriff! Yvette went into the house. Pauline followed and watched as she pulled an icepack out of the freezer, grabbed a dishtowel to wrap it in and went down the hall to retrieve the heating pad.

"Thanks. Now, where will I find this son of yours?" Pauline had been in much tougher situations in her own home. She put her calm, non-judgmental face on, parted her lips slightly and pulled them into a little smile. "Wish me luck."

"Last door on the left down that hallway. Want me to follow in case he gives you any grief?"

"No. If he's in a mood, I will just leave. I'll be fine." Pauline took a deep breath. "I've seen this one before."

Yvette knew she was referring to her home again. She knew Biggie to get into fights when he was drunk. Not so much in recent years, but twenty years ago he was a big bully.

Pauline knocked on Chance's bedroom door. Chance responded with a loud, angry response. "What?"

Pauline, in a calm but firm voice, responded.

"It's Pauline…" He interrupted before she could finish.

"Leave me alone. I don't want to talk about it."

"Hey, me neither. You're already paying the price. I want to put a heating pad on your shoulder for a bit and then some ice."

"Just leave it at the door. I'll take care of it." Chance wasn't backing down. He'd put himself in this position and didn't need anyone babying him.

"Sure thing. I'll be back out tomorrow, same time. Call me if you need anything before then."

That was it. That was all Pauline could do. She laid the heating pad and ice pack down on the floor in front of his door and backed away.

"Well, that was fun." She said to Yvette as she passed through the kitchen to leave.

"I'm sorry, honey. He shouldn't be taking anything out on you."

"No, it's okay. It happens. I'll try again to-morrow. See you then."

"Don't forget—Saturday. And ask your sweet momma, okay?"

"You've got it. See you tomorrow. Take care."

Pauline headed home, but at the last minute took the turn to the dude ranch. She had met

Bella at the house one day when she was working with Chance. Bella had invited her to stop by the dude ranch for coffee or a drink some day. Today seemed like a mighty fine day for a girl chat.

11

———

"Hey Bella!" Pauline called out. She hadn't been to the dude ranch before, but expected to find Bella in the dining hall at the center of the parking lot. The door was open so she let herself in.

"Well, hello Pauline! How are you doing? Great to see you!" Bella held flour-covered hands up bent at the elbow, and gave Pauline a quick hug.

"You out seeing Chance today?"

Pauline couldn't reveal much, but knew Yvette would freely share with Bella the afternoon's happenings. "Well, he cancelled our session after I got out here so I had some free time and thought I would stop by and say hi."

"How sweet is that? I'm working on dinner

here for the guests. Pull up a stool and chat with me. My hands are dirty or I'd pour you a drink. You can get it yourself, if you don't mind. There's coffee there in the lobby and some wine over here. We need to open the wine for dinner anyway. Go ahead, open a bottle there, if you want." Bella flipped a chicken breast in the flour and spice mixture and placed it in the hot pan.

"Sure smells good in here. I keep hearing what a great chef you are."

"Well, there's plenty here, how about you stay and join us?"

"Are you sure? Will you have enough if I stay?"

Bella laughed. "Oh, girl, I've always got extra. You're welcome anytime."

"What can I do to help?"

"You can pull those butter dishes out of the chiller and put one on each table. I've got some potato rolls rising. It'll be best if that butter softens some before dinner. Otherwise, open those wines. One red and one white on each table and one red for the kitchen. Oh, unless you prefer white."

"Well, I rarely drink, but I enjoy the red wines."

"I knew I liked you. Soon as I get this

chicken seared and in the oven, I'll have a few minutes to join you. Pour two glasses, will ya?"

Pauline unwrapped the butter dishes and set one on each table.

"Put that little one in there, on the table, please." Bella nodded toward her office. "Marco and Jennifer will be down here to eat when they're done up at the greenhouse." Jennifer worked in Steve's greenhouse, often with Yvette. She watched Marco while Bella was working. He enjoyed being with Jennifer and Yvette.

"I think it's awesome that Marco gets to grow up out here. Does he like it?" Pauline had seen the boy with Jesse over at the home place. She laughed watching them together: Jesse with his long stride, usually a hand in his pocket and little Marco in his shadow, taking the longest steps he could, with the same hand in his own little jeans pocket.

"He loves it here. He rarely talks about life in the city anymore. These guys have taken him under their wing and let him do all kinds of things. He adores Yvette. He doesn't have any grandparents, so he thinks of her like I thought of my grandmother. She's his older friend that he can tell anything to, and ask for anything."

"It sounds like a sweet arrangement." Pauline didn't know Bella's story, how she came to be here in Buffalo Ridge, but she knew the Davies family all thought she was an angel. Pauline liked her.

"So, how are things going with Chance? I know you can't tell me the medical stuff but Steve mentioned the other day that he was a little concerned about him." Bella didn't want to pry into the Davies family and start any drama, but Steve's comments alarmed her.

"What was Steve's concern?"

"Well, he said Chance was more withdrawn and didn't come around as much. One day he asked him to come help him with the horses when Jesse wasn't available and Chance snapped at him. Told him he didn't need any charity work, or something like that."

"Yeah, I think we're all seeing some of that side of Chance. We're keeping an eye on it and may need to call in some specialists to tease out whether it's related to his head injury or just the circumstances he's landed in. I appreciate you keeping me posted if you notice it changing though, okay?"

"Absolutely. You know, the whole family is grateful for what you're doing. We've all noticed that Chance responds to you and you are helping him find his way through this situation. I hope he's treating you well."

"It's been good but there have been some days, like today, when I've gotten similar reactions from him so I'm not surprised to hear it." Pauline would like to tell Bella everything, like how every time Chance raised his voice she feels like that little girl who couldn't get up from the table until she had eaten the cold oatmeal her dad gave her for dinner while Mom was working. "You will sit right there girl, until you eat all of that food, even if it means you're sleeping with your face in it!" Pauline shuddered at the memory.

"Well, us girls don't have to worry about that now, do we? Cheers to the girls of Buffalo Ridge." Bella picked up her glass and Pauline did the same. They toasted, two strangers united by the ranch and the Davies boys. Bella felt the possibility of a friendship here. Pauline wondered if this is what it felt like to have a sister, someone to whisper secret thoughts to out of earshot of the family.

"Cheers." They took a sip, each lost in their own thoughts.

"Mom, Mom!" Marco ran in the front door of the dining hall. "I found an earthworm in the basil. See? I'm going to save it for fishing with Dan."

"Whoah! Stop right there, son!" Marco froze in place. Bella came out of the kitchen to look.

"Well, isn't that a plump one? Do you have a place to keep him? Someplace outside? You know you can't bring him into my kitchen." They'd already had similar discussions over the past several weeks, as he seemed to always find interesting insects and things in the gardens and elsewhere outside.

"Yes, there's a bait box 'specially made for keeping fishing worms in. Dan has it in his truck. Is he coming here for dinner?"

"Well, I'm not sure about that. Let me go find something you can keep it in until Dan can get it and then I want you to wash up for dinner, okay?" Bella turned to retrieve an empty oatmeal box from the trash. "Here, he'll like this."

"Come on Marco. Let's put some dirt in there with him and then he'll be ready for Dan." Jennifer smiled at Bella and turned Marco around by the shoulders to head back outside and take care of their business.

"Thanks Jen." Bella called after them.

"Now that's funny! I bet he's got something new every day for you to deal with."

"Several times a day and I love it. I mean, if we were still in Manhattan, do you think he would know anything about earthworms? Or gardening? And most importantly, he's learning about family. I know we are not part of the Davies family but they sure treat us well."

"You're dating Steve now though, right?" Pauline had heard all about the dating from Yvette and Chance. Apparently, Steve asked Marco for permission to date his mom. "The fact that Steve asked Marco to date you is the sweetest thing I've ever heard."

"Oh, you heard about that, did you? I just wonder what Steve would have done if I said no.'" Bella was shaping dough into dinner rolls. "Not that I ever would have. He is all I could ever dream of in a guy. We work together, and for some people that doesn't work. I know from my last… well, Marco's Dad. But for Steve and I, we're like hand in glove. We have a lot of fun, at work and off."

"That sounds so wonderful, Bella. It's good to see him so happy and wonderful that you've made this transition to country life and found the bonus babe. I like it." Pauline loved a happy ending, even though she hadn't seen many. She devoured happy books when she was a teen, while her classmates were dating and partying. It had become a safe place for her, to get lost in a story.

"Well, it looks like the guests are getting

ready for dinner. You care to help me some more?"

"Of course. I'm sorry, I didn't mean to distract you from your work."

"Oh heavens, it's great to have someone to talk with. I just need to get these appetizers set out there in the lobby. Steve will take care of the drinks when he comes in. He'll be happy to see you."

Pauline washed her hands and gathered up the platters of meats and cheeses, olives and vegetables with dip. "These are beautiful, Bella. It's like a food painting."

Bella laughed. "I'm the crudités princess. I love crisp, colorful vegetables. I learned if I arrange them just right I can get guests excited about eating them. Most of these are from Steve's garden."

"I've done nothing like this. No wonder they call you the calorie queen."

"They call me what?" Bella hadn't heard this before. She wasn't sure she liked it.

"Yeah. Yvette says your food is so good she's gained ten pounds since you came."

"Speaking of Yvette." Bella nodded toward the front of the building with the big picture windows. Dan, Yvette and Chance were climbing out of Dan's pickup.

"Oh no. I'm afraid I may not be welcome here. I should go." Pauline felt a burn in her stomach. She didn't want to upset Chance. He had told her to go and here she was. "Damn!" she swore silently. "He probably thinks I'm over here gossiping about him."

"Well, if it isn't the two prettiest ladies in Buffalo Ridge… besides my lovely wife here." Dan pulled Yvette in close and gave her a kiss on the cheek.

"Good catch Dan, but you're right. They are two radiant beauties right there. Good to see you both." Yvette walked up to the serving window. "Anything I can do to help you gals out? Hope you don't mind Bella. I just don't have enough steam to whip up a meal tonight."

"You know it's no problem, Yvette. What I would like you to do is go on over there, pour yourself a drink, and put your feet up. Meanwhile, Marco has an earthworm for Dan. Maybe you can facilitate the transfer." Bella smiled at Yvette and nodded toward Marco who was outside with Jennifer.

"Hey Pauline, can I talk to you out here?" Chance called across the room then opened the screen door to walk out on the porch.

"What's that about?" Bella looked to her new friend.

"I don't know but I'm going to go find out. Thanks for the wine."

"Yeah, sure. Anytime. I mean that, you hear?"

BELLA NEEDED a friend here on the Plains, like her friend Angela in Manhattan. She wanted someone she could confide in, and someone who knew the people and the area. A little inside scoop would be helpful once in a while so she didn't step all over herself. She had already done that with Suzie Waldon, wife of the CEO of the largest business in town. Bella was in Buffalo Ridge one day with Yvette to pick up some things at the local country market. As they were standing in line to check out, she commented to Yvette that all the tourists coming to town clogged the roads like a gay pride parade in New York's Greenwich Village. The annual parade was one of the largest parades in the nation; while the visitors brought a lot of color, the locals didn't all care for the extra traffic. When Bella said it, Yvette's eyes grew wide. Suzie Waldon was checking out in front of them and she turned around and stared. "Well, that's one of the most unique descriptions I've ever heard about our little town."

She reached her hand out to Bella. "Pleased to meet you. I'm Suzie Waldon. You may have heard of my husband, Billy Waldon, the head of the business bringing all those tourists to town."

Bella's face burned with embarrassment. "Pleased to meet you ma'am. I meant no disrespect."

"None taken. I rather like a good gay pride parade myself." Suzie smiled tensely. "Who is your friend, Yvette? No, wait. I saw you out at the grand opening of the dude ranch, didn't I? You're that wonderful chef who came in from New York to help Steve out. Bella, right? Oh, Bella, what a find you were! Any time you want to talk pride parades or Madison Avenue, you call me. Yvette has my number."

Suzie took her bag from the checkout counter and walked away. Yvette and the grocery clerk, Lindsay, looked at each other and burst out laughing.

"You should have seen your face, Bella! Brighter than that tomato there in your cart." Lindsay pushed the groceries through the line and across the scanner.

"I'm mortified." Bella wasn't laughing.

"Oh honey, Suzie's a wonderful woman.

Look, you can see her through the front window there." Yvette pointed out the window toward the parking lot. Sure enough, Suzie was getting into her car with a huge smile across her face. "She liked that one, she really did."

"Honey, Suzie is real people just like us," she explained. "She got thrown into this awkward position through her husband's job. He has to hire and then fire the locals who work down at the business and that's made it hard for Suzie to have a lot of friends. She has some great friends, but she has to be careful. She really means it. She wants you to call her. Let's have her out to the ranch one day next week. She would love that."

Pauline joined Chance on the deck. He turned on her quickly. "Just what do you think you're doing here, Pauline? Telling Bella and all the family about my business?"

"No, I…"

Pauline tried to explain but Chance kept talking, through gritted teeth. He raised his finger and pointed it at her. "I should call Jackson and tell him you're violating my rights, telling everyone about my treatment. That's it, Pauline, you're fired."

Pauline felt the sting of his words in her chest. She knew better than to challenge him here. Guests were arriving. It would be better if she left now. "Understood. You take care Chance."

On the way home she called Jackson and explained the situation. He was understanding and reassuring. "I'm sorry, Pauline. I think it's best that you not try to work with Chance. I'll talk to Yvette about coming into the clinic an extra time every week. Meanwhile, like I told you before, there's ample work in your area. In fact, I've got a pleasant young man recovering from heart surgery. He needs some cardiac rehab but he can't drive yet and he's single, so there's no one to bring him in regularly. It's about the same number of hours you were working with Chance. What do you think?"

"Sure, that sounds good. Is he around here?" Pauline enjoyed having one foot in work. She would need to work full time again one day. Besides, the extra money helped her feel productive.

"He's in Weston. That's just about ten miles from you, right?"

"That's right. Can I call you for the details tomorrow? I don't have a pen with me. Better yet, can you put it all in the secure messaging portal and I can retrieve it there?"

"Absolutely. I'll call him and let him know you'll be there tomorrow, say about 2:00?"

"Yes, that will be perfect."

"Okay, I'll let you know if that doesn't work for him and we can set a different time. Thanks for the call, Pauline. I appreciate the heads-up in case he calls in with a complaint. But, you and I both know he was just blowing off steam. I believe there are natural consequences for that behavior and his consequence is that he doesn't get to work with you any more right now."

"Thanks for your understanding Jackson. I look forward to working with the new client."

Once home, Pauline sent a text to Yvette. *Sorry, something came up and I won't be able to go to the spa. You girls have fun!* She was numb to this type of disappointment; it was all she had ever known.

12

Curtis Stamm was a name Pauline knew from high school. He was the neighboring town's star athlete, setting records in track and basketball. A sign advertising the family's Charolais bulls was planted along the interstate so passers-by could see it when driving east into Buffalo Ridge. Curtis was the eighth generation to ranch this land of rolling grasslands, flat hay ground and on the far south, the western edge of the rugged Badlands.

Pauline had never driven to this area and was awed by the peace that greeted her. She had always lived in Buffalo Ridge and although rural, because she didn't live on a farm or ranch, she wasn't a country girl. Her life centered around the small town until she left after graduating from high school. She rarely visited schoolmates' homes where she might have learned to ride a horse or bottle-feed a calf.

Curtis' home was attractive. It was a sprawling ranch design with cedar siding and a glass prow front facing the south. A large deck extended out from the front and a giant cedar tree shaded a portion of the yard. Free-range chickens pecked at the ground behind the house. A shiny fifth-wheel trailer rested next to the garage and a dually pickup sat in the driveway. There were outbuildings scattered around the area.

Pauline grabbed her clipboard and dynamometer to test her new patient's strength as a baseline for his treatment. Before she could knock, the door opened, and a slightly winded but handsome Curtis Stamm opened the door. Pauline had no preconceived notion of what Curtis would look like, but nothing she imagined would have prepared her for the cheery strawberry blonde with piercing bright blue eyes who greeted her.

"You must be Pauline." His voice was rough, probably from months of using oxygen and intubation from his recent surgery.

"I am Pauline Whyte, Curtis. It's very nice to meet you." She shook his strong hand.

"Please, come on in." Curtis opened the door wide so Pauline could join him in the living room.

"You have a beautiful place out there." Pauline found the house to be as tidy as the outside and modern, without the usual western tchotchke she expected from a bachelor living out on the plains.

"Thank you. I'm very blessed to have a small slice of heaven, right here. Can I get you some water, or coffee maybe?"

"Pauline held up her water bottle. "I'm set. How about you? Is this a good time for you to meet, get some history and do a little therapy?"

"Sure, sure. I'm not going anywhere." Curtis smiled.

"Fair enough. Let's start there. So, you live here alone. Who helps you get groceries and go to the doctor?" Pauline was curious whether he had a girlfriend or an ex-wife that helped him out but she also needed the information for her intake form.

"Yeah, my brother Calvin, his wife Brenda, and their kids live just over the hill there. All this land used to be our parents', before they passed away. So, they live just over there about three miles. They have a sick baby. I mean, like terminally sick. She won't live to go to school even, so my sister-in-law spends most of her time caring for Sarah. Once a week she has a service that comes in and stays with her so Brenda can do the shopping. She stops by here and gets my list. Bless her heart, she usually has some leftovers frozen for me to put in the freezer and eat during the week.

"Well, it sounds like all of you are facing some big challenges. Do you feel that's enough help for you to get through your recovery?"

"Sure do. There are a lot of church people who stop by and help too. A neighbor from up north came by yesterday and mowed the yard. I hired a hand to see after the cattle until I'm back on my feet. Calvin will take me to the doctor. Fortunately, I don't have to go often now."

Curtis told Pauline his history and recent status following aortic valve replacement. Prior to surgery he was oxygen dependent and now, although he was slow and his sternum still ached from the surgery, he didn't need oxygen and felt his stamina returning.

"It will be better than new in three months or so. Pauline, I could sure use your help to get some strength back. I couldn't do a lot in those six months before surgery so I know I've lost some muscle."

They did strength testing and some exercises.

"It's clear that you were strong before all this started, Curtis. I'm looking forward to working with you to get that strength back and I can tell you're eager to get there too."

They set a schedule for him to do exercises on his own. She would return three times each week for the first two weeks and then they would reevaluate.

"I'm looking forward to it, Pauline. Thanks for coming all the way out here. I know it's a drive for you."

"It's not bad at all and I love the scenery. You take care, Curtis, and I will see you in two days."

Pauline returned to town to be with her parents for the evening. Even though he was barely responsive, her father always reached his hand out from under the covers when she came in the room. He kept her connected, even on those days she just wanted to run away from it all and start over with a new name, a new history, and big dreams. She had never had any dreams and no place to run to, but she had read about such things in a book and it seemed the right thing to do.

As she sat vigil with her father, a text chime interrupted her thoughts. The text read *So sorry you can't join us hun. Would love to have you come back. Give Chance a couple of days to cool down then he'll be ready. I'm sure of it.* Pauline hoped to see Yvette around town, Bella, too, but she would not go back to work with Chance.

She texted back. *I'll be working with a new client. So sorry.* Pauline knew Yvette wouldn't ask who the client was but in this small community, even ten, fifteen miles away, through the church ladies or the coffee drinkers, she would find out.

———

Pauline's work with Curtis was a dream. He was ultra compliant and determined to return to optimal condition. "I have things to accomplish, Pauline. These cattle don't take care of themselves. Winter's coming and I will need to get feed to them and chop the ice in their water. You know, there's always something to do. I've got equipment to maintain so it's ready in the spring… I'm sorry, all this ranch talk must be boring you."

Pauline smiled. "No, not at all. I love seeing a man passionate about his work and I learn something every time I talk with you."

THREE WEEKS into her work with Curtis, she heard again from Yvette via text with Bella copied. *Having a family dinner at the dude ranch on Friday night. Hope you can join us. We ALL miss you.*

Pauline thought about the invitation. Her dad was the same. Her mom was hanging in there. The hospice staff told them they had seen this before, where someone just lingers, their willpower stronger than their body. They could not predict how much longer he would hang on but they strongly encouraged Pauline and Loretta to live their lives.

She wanted to see Yvette and Bella. It was a small town. She couldn't avoid them forever. Hopefully Chance knew enough to stay away if she irritated him. *Thank you. I'll be there. What can I bring? Let me know what time.*

Bella sent the response, and in it she reassured Pauline that Chance had turned his anger elsewhere. They would gather at five for cocktails then dinner. There was no need for Pauline to bring a thing.

Pauline showed up on Saturday night with flowers for Bella, a hostess gift of sorts. She hadn't seen her or spoken to her since she was essentially thrown out without the opportunity to say goodbye.

Bella took the bouquet and threw her arms

around Pauline. "Oh Pauline, it's so wonderful to see you again! Come. Keep me company in the kitchen. The others are running late so it's just Marco and I."

"Hey, Marco. How are you doing?" She gave him a high-five.

"I'm grrrreat! I'm in school now and I have so many new friends. There are too many to count but there's Annie Jo, Alison, Marcus... that's really close to my name and he's my best friend..."

"Honey, you don't need to tell Pauline all the kids in your class."

"I'm happy to hear you're enjoying it, Marco. Is Mrs. Foster your teacher?"

Marco raised his head and looked at Pauline with giant eyes. "How did you know that? Mrs. Foster is the best teacher ever!"

"Well, he's excited." Pauline turned to Bella who was handing her a glass of red wine.

"That boy is always excited about something or another. Cheers! To friends." Bella looked into Pauline's eyes, wanting her to know she meant it. They were friends.

"Friends." Pauline nodded and smiled. "So, what's news around here? Tourist season is winding down. What's keeping you busy out here now?"

"I have to tell you, Steve is a marketing guru. There was a National Grasslands conference and for a week that group filled up the cabins. They only ate two meals a day here so it felt like a mini vacation. Then, there are all these hunting seasons. Deer with a bow and arrow and deer with rifles, pheasant… you know better than I do. Steve, he's got something lined up almost every week. I finally said I wanted some time off, so he closed the calendar for Christmas week."

Pauline laughed. "Oh, that's funny."

"What? What are you laughing about?" Bella looked confused.

Pauline furrowed her brows and tightened her lips. "Did he bother to tell you about the hayrides and sleigh rides they do at the ranch during December? I'm guessing you're going to get roped into cookie making with Santa and hot chocolate with Rudolph."

Bella sighed. "No, he sure didn't mention that. Guess we'll have something to talk about tomorrow when we're back at work. For tonight, let's party! I hope you like fish. We're having wild salmon and halibut sent by a guest from Alaska and some locally grown good-looking filet mignon." She looked around the kitchen to take inventory and decide her next steps. "And I've got the best chocolate cake for dessert. Sorry, I shouldn't spoil all the surprises. Will you grab those limes, lemons and olives? I'll take the appetizers and we can have a seat out by the fireplace."

Pauline picked up the dishes and her wine. She followed Bella. "What's the special occasion?"

"What do you mean?"

"Well, why are you all getting together for dinner tonight?"

"Oh, this? We do this at least once a month. Usually it's more often but not always here. Sometimes Steve cooks up at his place or Yvette and Dan will cook. Steve is mostly a grill cook. I guess he could have cooked this meal up there but hey, we're here, let's enjoy it. Looks like they're pulling in now."

Pauline drew in a deep breath.

"Relax girl, there's nothing for you to worry about. I've got your back." Bella reached out to her friend and squeezed her forearm.

Pauline looked at Bella with a hint of panic on her face. "Thanks."

"There are my girls." Yvette was the first to enter, gliding across the floor as fast as her legs would take her. She wrapped her arms around

Pauline and squeezed her tight. "Pauline, it's so great to see you."

Dan and Jesse followed. Dan gave Pauline a big hug and Jesse shook her hand. Jesse was always kind to Pauline. "Pauline, it's good to see you. How's your dad?"

"He's still hanging on though his doctors can't figure out how. At least he seems comfortable. Thanks for asking."

Steve and Chance were the last to join the party. By the time they came inside, Pauline was on her second glass of wine. She couldn't remember a time when she had more than one glass of wine. She felt warm and loose, shared jokes with the others and was more relaxed than usual in a group setting.

Steve greeted Pauline with a one-armed hug then took a step to Bella and bent down to plant a gentle kiss on her lips. Chance followed and gave Pauline a hug, his injured arm reaching around to her lower back. He caught her ear during the hug and whispered a message. "Can we talk outside?"

Pauline pulled back and looked Chance directly in the eye. "That didn't go so well the last time, so right now, I'm going to say no."

Chance squeezed her hand. "Fair enough. Can I get you a drink?"

It surprised Pauline that Chance didn't stomp off when she didn't acquiesce to him. She was trying to hold boundaries, but it was hard, especially after drinking. What she wanted to do was follow him to the deck and throw herself at him.

Dinner was delightful, both in food and company. The family reviewed the week and talked a little about the week to come. They asked Pauline about her dad and how she was doing. She updated them on Biggie's status, which was grim. Pauline drank water with dinner. She didn't like feeling fuzzy after drinking two glasses of wine.

"Pauline, I hear you're working with Curtis Stamm." Yvette was sure to discover her client's identity. "It's such a shame that a star athlete has gotten so sick."

"Well, as you all know, I can't talk about my clients. But I can tell you that any client I am working with at this time is showing great progress and I'll not be needed indefinitely." Pauline smiled at the group and raised her water glass. "Cheers to the chef."

The table all raised their glasses and clinked in Bella's honor. That was the thanks she loved and the thanks that made nights like this all worth it.

"Pauline, would you help me clear the table? Then I've got a fabulous chocolate dessert? Who would like coffee?" Everyone at the table raised a hand, except Marco, who by now was getting sleepy.

"Marco honey, come sit with me while Pauline and Mommy clear the table." Yvette took him to the sofa near the fireplace and sat with him. They talked about his day and school. That boy was never short on words.

"Here, let me help." Chance stood and gathered dirty dishes to carry to the kitchen. He caught up with Pauline. "Hey, Pauline. I know I owe you an apology, and I am sorry but I would like to talk to you, as my friend, not my therapist."

Pauline looked at him. He hadn't called her a friend before and it took her by surprise.

"Okay Chance, but not tonight, ok? Let's have coffee tomorrow."

"Sure, looking forward to it."

13

———

Chance stood as Pauline walked into the Pony Espresso coffee shop. "Good morning, Pauline. Thanks for joining me. What can I get you?"

"Good morning Chance. How about a chai tea, with almond milk, please." Pauline slipped off her jacket and sat at the table near the front window, overlooking Main Street while Chance placed their order.

He returned to the table with both coffees and a paper bag with a slice of banana bread for each of them. "Here. Thought maybe you would like a little bite to eat, too."

"Look at you, carrying with both hands. Looking good there, Chance." Their eyes met. She bit her lip.

"Yeah, I'm doing pretty good, but I'm sure I would recover faster if I was still working with you." Chance studied her for a reaction.

"I'm sure Jackson has you on a good course for recovery. Anyway, I'm pretty booked up, as you know." Pauline heard herself, distancing from Chance, wary of his intentions for the meeting this morning.

"Pauline, I was so wrong to accuse you the way I did. I know you're far too professional to be talking about my treatment behind my back. Besides, around the ranch there are no secrets."

"So I've noticed. I wonder how your mom found out who I was working with?"

"I'm sure that was church lady gossip. Even though Curtis lives out of town, the church ladies cross town boundaries all the time." Chance shook his head. His mom didn't intend to be a gossip, but she sure was in the middle of it often.

"I suppose that's true. I guess I have flown under the radar so long that I haven't been at the center of such gossip."

"Well, you may not know it but there is talk about us." Chance smiled and wagged his finger indicating the two of them.

"Wait. Back it up. Us? What do you mean?"

Pauline set her coffee down and looked at Chance, waiting for an answer.

"Well, I mean people saw us out together and assumed we were dating." Chance took a gulp of coffee, set down his cup and reached over to cover her hand with his. "Pauline, would that be such a bad thing?"

"What, if people thought we were dating, or if we were dating?"

"Sorry, Pauline. I'm having a hard time getting it out. I had it all written down but you know, my memory isn't what it used to be."

"You wrote it down?"

"Sure. That journal you gave me, thank you again. I've been using it, like you said. I've worked on this conversation for a week or more. It looked good on paper, I think."

"Chance, just stop thinking from here…" Pauline reached over and gently put her hand on his temple. "… And think from here." She moved her hand to his chest. "Take a deep breath… let it out… then start over."

"Okay, here we go." Chance cleared his throat and shifted in his chair. He leaned into the table and looked into her eyes. "Pauline, I really like you, and I don't mean as my caregiver, but as a woman. As someone I'd like to date. Pauline, would you go out with me?"

Pauline blushed and looked down. The advice she gave Chance hung heavy in the air. Her head rattled on about the hurt from man's anger and oppression, yet her heart longed for the touch of this man. Could she ever trust enough? She uncrossed her legs, stretched them out and crossed her ankles before tucking them under her chair. "Can we talk about what happened Chance? About your anger?"

"Sure. There were some things going on that you didn't know about, and this whole thing has frustrated me because I can't do anything on my own. There's no excuse, though. I should never have talked to you like that."

"Well we agree on that, at least." Pauline sat back in her chair and crossed her arms. She'd heard apologies for outbursts before and they were always empty. They didn't stop the rants.

"Yeah, and I talked to Jackson. I told him it was all my fault, and you did nothing wrong. I understand why you didn't want to work with me again. Honestly, I think it's for the best. I don't think you would ever consider going out with me on a real date if you were still giving me therapy. You're too much of a professional for that." Chance paused. He took a bite of his bread and washed it down with coffee, hoping what he was saying made sense.

"Well, thank you. I think professional boundaries are important and honestly, I may have crossed that line when I suggested we go to the rodeo."

"Hey, no! That was a fantastic thing. Let me tell you what happened. So, remember we saw old Tom Hamm at the rodeo? I'm not sure I told you, but he was my mentor when I started bull riding. It's because of him I've had the success I have. He opened his home and his stables to me. I practically lived with him when I was, I'd say ten to about fifteen. We went to different events."

"You said you trained with him, but I guess I never understood to what extent."

"Well, anyway, I went to see him, like he asked out there at the rodeo grounds that day. He told me he's dying. Every day now he gets weaker and sicker but he's so damned ornery he won't let anyone come in and take care of him. Pauline, he offered me his bull riding school business and his ranch."

"He what? Are you kidding me?"

"Yeah, and that was weighing on my mind that day when I went flying off the handle at you. Again, it's not an excuse, just context." He paused again, waiting for Pauline to absorb what he told her.

"You know, he was like a second dad to me and that was some tough news to hear. I knew something was up when I pulled into his place. He was always so meticulous, but it's clear now that he hasn't had the energy to keep things up to his standard. The house needs a coat of paint and the equipment needs repair. He had a horse out there he's supposed to be breaking, but he just can't do it."

"Wow, that's a lot going on Chance. I had no idea."

"Yeah, yeah, you couldn't have known. Really, I'm not trying to make up excuses. I should have found a better way to talk this through but I guess I just wasn't ready. My good buddy had just given me bad news and then offered me the world but I wasn't sure my broken body would be any better for the place than old Tom is."

"So, are you still thinking about his offer?"

"No, no, I'm not." Chance paused. He was still settling in with his decision.

"The day after I met with Tom, I saw the surgeon and Jackson. They were really excited about how I was healing, but I wanted to be one hundred percent healed, right then and there."

"But Chance…"

"I get it now, that wasn't realistic. But, I'm Chance Davies. I'm the king of the rodeo and I get things my way. At least I did until I met Big Brutus. One day, they tell me, I will be thankful about all this but I'm still not there."

"Right. That's asking a lot. So, what do you think now? I mean about Tom's offer."

"Well, after I blew up at you, I sort of locked myself in my room for a few days and did a lot of thinking." Chance paused and looked around to see that nobody else could hear him. He leaned in closer. "To be honest Pauline, and I have told no one this, I spent most of that time crying and praying. I prayed for some understanding and some vision."

They sat in silence while he swallowed back his emotion. His voice started with a crackle. "So, I told old Tom yes. I've already been reorganizing the school and working with Steve to set up some longer riding schools where the students can get room and board up there at his place. Tom has an indoor arena at his place. It's not real big but big enough to hold classes year round. We're still working with his lawyer on the terms of the ranch. He won't agree to take my money…"

"What? How could that be? Why wouldn't he want to be paid for his property?"

"Well, he sees me as his heir. He has nobody

else. He was an orphan and never had any kids. He says I was the son he never had, and this is the way he wants it." Chance ran his hands through his hair. The thought of not paying for the ranch didn't sit well with him. It wasn't the way he was raised, to take something for nothing.

"Chance, it's a dying man's wish that you take over his place. If you can't come to an agreement on payments, you could make other agreements, like hosting an equine therapy program or donating to a designated charity or something."

"I never thought about that. Those are great ideas. I'll think about it. We meet with his lawyer again in a few days so I could bring that up." He looked at her, reached over and squeezed her hand. "See, that's why I need you close, Pauline. You're the smart one. You're also very beautiful."

"Now I know you've lost it, Chance. Give me a break."

"I'm sorry, what..." Chance paused. He didn't understand her reaction. "Pauline, you are beautiful and I have fallen for you. Now, back to my original question. Will you go out with me, beautiful Pauline?" His hand reached up and he ran it gently along the side of her face.

The pause was brief before her plump lips broke into a smile. It was her heart that spoke. "It would delight me to go out with you, Chance Davies, king of the rodeo."

14

"Hey babe, will you hand me that hand saw over there? I need to cut this board down." Pauline retrieved the saw and held it out to Chance. One of their first dates, two days after the coffee shop visit, was to fix fences at Tom's place.

"Thanks. This isn't what I thought we would do on a date but I appreciate your help."

Pauline smiled. "It's okay. Just so we get to spend time together, it's all good."

Chance pulled her close. "Kiss me, Pauline."

He bent to cover her lips with his. Time passed yet stood still. "You taste sweet. What's your secret?"

Pauline smiled and looked up into his eyes. "No secret. That's just me."

Chance spotted Tom out of the corner of his eye, standing on the front porch, waving for the two to come into the house. "Let's go see what Tom wants."

Hand-in-hand they walked to the house.

"You two lovebirds want some coffee? Got some cookies here, too, from Mrs. Brooks there in town." Tom held a tin of homemade cookies, jiggling as his hand shook. "Damn tremor. Like everything, it's worse."

They each took a cookie to lighten the load. "How's it looking out there?"

"Looks good, Tom. Just adding a brace to that fence there by the gate. I think we can move the herd in and sort 'em." Tom had nearly two hundred cow-calf pairs and all would go to market, unless he could convince Chance to take them.

"Have a seat there." Tom nodded to the kitchen table. He pushed his pill bottles to the side so they could put their coffee down.

Tom dropped a stack of papers on the table. "Missy, maybe you can talk some sense into this boy. If I take them cattle to the sale barn, when I die the state will get that money. In them papers there, the attorney showed some other ways to manage so not so much of the money goes to waste and it could be used for better things. Just take them, will ya, and think about it."

Tom's stoop was worse. He got winded quickly. That outburst used all his energy for the day.

"Yes, I will talk to him about it, Tom," Pauline reassured him. "Can I ask you, have you ever thought about other ranch businesses you would have grown or invested in out here?"

"Hmm… come to think of it, there was a time Mrs. Nora Harney, you know, down there where 82 meets the 264, anyway, seems she had a niece or something who worked with those kids with challenges. What did she say? I think it was like autism and something. Anyway, she had some horses specially trained to work with them kids and she wondered, since I have the little arena down there, if she could rent the space and have some lessons down there. It was when I was startin' to get sick and I just… well, I didn't give her an answer."

"What would you think of Chance doing something like that?"

"Well, hell yeah, if it's gonna help them kids. I think that's the right thing to do, ya know… help them kids. They got a tough life, and the parents too."

"I'll look into it Tom. It sounds like a worthy cause."

"Would warm my heart some, son, if they got some good outta it." Tom looked away, but not before Pauline saw a lone tear escape from his eye.

The coffee break ended. Pauline and Chance returned to the fence to finish up, working quietly with much on their minds.

"Now, how about we take a little time for us? What would you like to do?" Chance looked at Pauline sitting beside him on the pickup seat.

"I want you to come to my house and meet my dad. He won't respond, probably, but it may be the only opportunity we have. He's stopped eating now so we're looking at just a few days and he'll be gone."

"I would love to do that. Do you want to grab a bite to eat first, or maybe after?"

"Let's stop by the house first. Shouldn't take long. Mom might be there, too."

From Tom's place it was only ten minutes to the Whyte's house. Her parents' old pickup was in the driveway. "Looks like Sherry, the hospice nurse is here." Pauline recognized her red Chevy.

The house was small, just two bedrooms. Biggie thought that was plenty for them since they only had one child. The front room was furnished sparsely. Biggie's recliner was obvious. Years of television watching from that chair were clear. Duct tape held the stuffing in the arms and seat where the naugahyde had worn through. The living room was open to the kitchen. It was well worn and dated but spotless. Biggie lay in the hospital bed in Pauline's room. Since he became bedridden, she slept on the couch with the flattened cushions.

"Hey Sherry. Hi Mom." The ladies had just changed Biggie and were tucking fresh sheets around him.

"Hi Dad. It's Pauline. I have a friend with me here." Biggie's hand crept out from under the covers toward her. His fingers were now frail and thin. Pauline took his hand in hers. "This is Chance Davies, Dad. He's my boyfriend."

Pauline felt a slight tension in her father's hand as he attempted to squeeze hers.

"Mom, this is Chance."

"Hi Chance. Pleasure to meet you. Again, actually. I met you at your mom's a long time ago, but you've sure grown up since then."

"Pleasure to meet you as well," Chance answered politely. "My memory's not the greatest right now, but Mom has spoken of you helping her out."

"How are things here?" Pauline looked to Shelly.

"His breathing is more shallow. We've giving him the morphine every hour so he doesn't have any discomfort."

"Mom, I'm going to go grab a bite to eat with Chance. Can we bring you anything? I'll be back right after that, okay?"

"I don't need a thing. I called in for work tonight. I don't want to leave your dad. Besides, it's not too busy down there." Her evening job was washing dishes at the Buffalo Diner. Some days they cancelled her shift, when it was too slow to justify her slim wages. The owners were local folks and were understanding of Loretta's situation.

Pauline's car was out at Buffalo Ridge Ranch so they decided just to drive out there to find something to eat. Neither of them felt like going out.

"Hey kids, how are you guys? Get the fence fixed?" Yvette was in the kitchen when they got there, canning carrot pickles from the last batch of carrots pulled from the garden for the season.

"Yeah, we sure did. We were just going to grab a quick bite. Do you have any of the lasagna left over? I'll just heat us up some."

"Have a seat and let me do it." Yvette pulled

the remnants of last night's lasagna from the fridge and turned the oven on. "So tell me, how's Tom doing?"

"He's not good Mom. He's losing strength. I don't understand how he thinks he can stay there by himself until he passes."

"Maybe he doesn't think that. Maybe he's thinking you'll be there, Chance. Do you think that's part of why he's pushing so hard for you to keep your money?"

"I thought about that and I will offer, but I don't think he's ready for a full-time live-in. I mean, I think it would be intrusive for him."

"You know, what you could do is pull the RV over there and just stay nearby." Yvette had run several scenarios through her head in recent weeks preparing for this conversation.

"I think that's a great idea, Yvette." Pauline perked up. She had been quiet, lost in her own thoughts.

When they finished eating Pauline wanted to go home rather than linger. She felt a need to be with her family.

"Here honey, take some of this to your mom. I saw her the other day and she's just wasting away."

"Thanks, Yvette. She'll appreciate it." Pauline took the container of salad and another of more lasagna. They exchanged hugs. "You take care now, Pauline."

Chance opened the door for her and walked with her to the car. He opened the car door, took the containers and placed them on the passenger seat. He reached for her and pulled her close in a long, warm hug before they kissed deeply. Both were hungry to have their anxieties and fears soothed by the touch of the other.

"See you tomorrow?" Chance would pass by the Whyte house on his way to Tom's.

"I'll see Curtis tomorrow, if things are stable at home." Pauline knew that stable was a relative term these days. Her dad could slip away at any moment, but she had sat by his bedtime and told him goodbye a hundred times already.

"Okay. Well, let's stay in touch. I could swing by with a hot chai, if nothing else. See you babe." As she tucked herself in the seat, he gently closed the car door.

The day shift hospice staff called in sick the next day so Pauline had to delay her visit to Curtis until late afternoon. Her dad had a fever. An infection had again taken over his body. His chest rattled as he breathed slowly. He no longer reached out to her when she came into the room and called out to him.

"I'll be back in a couple of hours Daddy."

Pauline reached down and kissed her father's heated forehead.

"Call me if you need anything." She spoke to the air between her mom and the afternoon nurse, Amy. It was hard to leave but she just couldn't stay here night and day waiting for her dad to stop breathing.

THERE WERE SO many things on her mind that the drive passed quickly. Before she knew it, she was pulling into Curtis's driveway.

Curtis had just finishing his prescribed walk. Today they would do some resistance training and some stretching. He still had pain in his sternum that kept his breathing and movement constrained. Pauline was working on building up his confidence with these motions so he could continue his healing journey without her. He had achieved maximum benefit in good time.

"Good to see you Pauline."

"You, too, Curtis. How was the walk?" She unzipped her jacket and hung it on the hook next to the door. The fall days were getting chilly fast.

"Six miles. Feels great."

"That's fantastic. How does the cool air feel in your lungs?"

"So far, so good. I'm sure when it gets cooler it will be harder but I have a mask I can use."

"Excellent. Now, today we will work on some of those movements you need to hoist yourself up into the big tractor. You know the ones, where you have to stretch and pull yourself up."

Curtis made a tense face. "To be honest, that sounds a little painful."

"Right, and that's why we need to do this work. We don't want those muscles there in your chest to get bound up. We need to stretch and strengthen them so you can do your work. I know that's important to you."

"You're right, it is. The guys who have been helping me out need to get back to their own work full time. I've already got a lot of paybacks piled up for those fellas, and ladies."

"So, expect to feel some pulling and stretching but a sharp, stabbing pain means we've gone too far. So let's not go there." Pauline pulled out a resistance band and showed the exercises. He repeated the sequence of exercises, then took notes so that he could do them on his own until she returned to work with him.

"I'll plan to be back in three days. If something comes up, I'll let you know and we can reschedule. We'll start wrapping up your treatment and space out my visits further over the next two weeks."

"So, you think I'm ready to graduate? I can't thank you enough for all your help, Pauline. You've been a real godsend to me." Curtis moved in to give her a hug. Pauline backed away and held her hand out.

"It's always good to see you Curtis. Keep up the good work." She took his hand and let him shake hers.

The near hug from Curtis unsettled Pauline. Had she misread the move? Maybe he hugged everyone. She didn't think so. He had never hugged her goodbye before. It was uncharacteristic, but maybe she was reading too much into it. What if Curtis liked her like that? Would she be good with that?

15

"Yes, I need to arrange for a cremation. Yes ma'am. The deceased is my father. His name is Robert Whyte spelled w—h—y—t—e. That's right. I don't know if it matters for your paperwork or anything, but he was known as Biggie. Nobody called him Robert... Thank you ma'am. We'll watch for the van then. Thank you."

Biggie had waited for Pauline to return home from Curtis's therapy before he took his last breath. Loretta, Pauline and the hospice nurses were there as his breaths became more and more shallow until eventually they ceased. Loretta and Pauline went right into clean-up mode, packing the leftover medications and supplies into bags and handing them to the hospice team to take away. They made arrangements with the after-hours staff at the medical equipment supplier to retrieve the hospital bed with its special mattress that had cushioned her dad's body and the oxygen concentrator.

The nurses and Loretta lovingly prepared Biggie's body as they waited for the cremation service. Loretta hugged her husband one last time and kissed his face. As inevitable as it was, they were sad to see him go. He had been a powerful force in their world.

After hospice left and the cremation service carried away Biggie's body, Pauline and Loretta sat quietly at the kitchen table, drinking tea and making a list of people to contact. The list was short. Biggie didn't have much family. He alienated many over the years and the remaining ones he knew were older and not in good health. Loretta's family wouldn't care. They had written her off years ago when Biggie dragged her to Buffalo Ridge. Pauline never did get to meet the maternal side of her family.

Pauline had written an obituary with her father early in his illness. It was short and simple, mentioning his family and his military service. He insisted there would be no funeral and they would bury his cremains at the National Veteran's Cemetery, marked with a simple white headstone of the fallen soldiers. "That's the least they can do for me and my family," he had said.

"How are you doing Mom?" Pauline looked to Loretta, the small woman who had always lived under the thumb of someone, first her own father and then Biggie.

"I'm okay. We knew this was coming, right?" She got up and washed her teacup.

"Why don't you go get some rest. I'll leave a message at the motel to let them know you won't be in to clean rooms in the morning. They probably don't have many anyway."

"That's all right. I don't think I can sleep. Think I'll just watch some TV."

Pauline watched her mom sit down in the small recliner beside the oversized recliner her father practically lived in for years. She watched as her mom stared at the screen, occasionally reaching over to Biggie's chair and patting the arm, as if Biggie was still sitting there and she was patting his arm.

Pauline needed some sleep. She didn't feel like contacting Chance, or anyone, to tell them about Biggie. She needed to sit with it for a while first, let it really sink in that her dad was gone and her mother's rock was not there to prop her up. She worried that her mother wouldn't be able to move forward from this, that she would do exactly what she was doing now. Work and come home to an empty house. Sit beside an empty chair, forgetting to eat and take care of herself.

After a short night of sleep Pauline woke to chimes from her phone as text messages landed. Yvette's was the first to come through. *Honey, we heard about Biggie's passing. So sorry for your loss. Let us know about services and what we can do to help you and Loretta. Love Yvette and ALL.* Chance followed with a hurried message. *Sorry about your dad. Call me.*

Pauline didn't feel like calling anyone. She felt that she could sleep for a week. A loud crash interrupted her thoughts. She popped out of bed to find her mom in the kitchen. She had pulled all the pots and pans out and was washing the cupboards. One of the cake tins had toppled off the pile on the tiny counter onto the badly scratched old linoleum floor.

"What's going on out here? Mom, did you get any sleep?" Pauline reached for the teakettle. It was lukewarm and had been on in the last hour.

"I slept. You know me, I've just got to keep busy."

"So when you get this done, what are you

going to do to keep busy? How about you and I go to the city Mom? Just get away for a couple of days." To Pauline, it felt like death and fear in the house. "I need some fresh air. I don't feel like I can breathe in here right now."

"Oh, honey, you know there'll be people stopping by and bringing food and passing on their condolences. They can't come to an empty house." She patted Pauline's hands, fingers woven tightly together, trying to maintain her composure. "Did you sleep okay?"

"No, Mom. I can't say I slept well. Between the banging in the kitchen and my text messages beeping, I don't feel like I got much sleep at all." Pauline was unusually irritable. She turned up the fire under the kettle.

By mid-morning Pauline's phone was ringing. The mortician needed more information. A rancher from up north had heard about Biggie's passing and wanted to know if the house would be for sale. His kids needed a place to stay when they started high school next year. The VA returned her call to discuss burial details and the burial benefits. Her phone beeped while she was on that call. After she hung up, she saw it was Chance. He called right back a few minutes later.

"You didn't call me. Sorry to hear about your dad." He sounded tense.

"Thanks. It's been kinda busy around here this morning. Sorry I couldn't get your call." She felt irritable and regretted apologizing for not getting the phone. She was busy, darn it.

"Want me to come over? Anything I can do?" Chance was eager to be of support but had work to do out at Tom's. Every day he found more and more broken down things to fix there. He had some doubts about taking on the place, but still wanted to be there for Tom in whatever way he could.

"No, thanks. I will hang here with Mom and handle some arrangements. Can I call you tomorrow?" Pauline didn't feel like talking. She felt like she was in a fog.

"Okay. 'Til then take care of yourself, my beautiful Pauline."

PAULINE WENT to her dad's tool drawer and gathered up the hammer and screwdriver. She set about tightening the hinges and knobs in the kitchen. As long as her mom was going to clean things up, she might as well lend a hand. The little projects turned into a major deep cleaning. The two worked in tandem, washing down the walls, cleaning out closets and doing their best to wash away the stink of illness and death. It was the only way they knew how to cope: keep the hands busy.

Pauline snuck down the street to the grocery store dumpster and returned with an armful of boxes. She set them up in the living room. "These over here are for trash Mom, and here, put the things to be donated. I'll call and have the charity service pick them up. And I'll have Gary's Quick Pick come over and haul away the trash. And he's taking that big old chair."

Loretta looked at her daughter. She didn't have the wherewithal to argue about the ratty old chair Biggie loved so much. It was probably for the better to get it out of here. "Well, that will leave a lot more space in this room then."

"We'll look at getting you some fancy new furniture Mom, if you're sure you want to stay here."

"Well, of course I will stay here. Where would you have me go, the Pioneer Park?"

"No, Mom. You don't need assisted living. I just mean this is an opportunity for you to re-evaluate what you want, where you want to be."

Loretta looked over the discarded items Pauline pulled from closets and cupboards, examining them for their remaining usefulness. "This place is all I've known. I haven't ever thought about being anywhere else. I don't have any people back on the rez. The only other place I've been outside South Dakota is Vegas and that was forty years ago. I've got no interest in living there."

By the end of the cleaning spree, the house held two beds, two dressers (mostly empty), a kitchen table with two chairs, and Loretta's recliner. The cupboards and closets held half the stuff they used to.

"We'll get you some new furniture, Mom, but I'm going to fix this ratty floor first." Loretta didn't protest.

When Loretta had cleaned every corner of the tiny house, she started tidying up the outside. She cleared useless stuff from the shed and straightened the flowerbeds.

***

AFTER A FEW DAYS, Pauline returned to work. She wrapped up her therapy with Curtis and took on two new clients. She begged out of seeing Chance for the first several days, mostly because she felt lost, uncertain of what her next step should be. Her mom would be okay financially without working, but she didn't know what to do with herself.

Chance became impatient and just showed up at Pauline's house one afternoon. People had come and gone repeatedly, bringing casseroles and sharing their condolences. It irritated Pauline to see him. She wanted to cocoon from the world and its realities. She was struggling with what she should do next. Living with her mother was not a long-term option. It was too dreary, quiet and sad around the house.

"Hey Chance, what's up?"

Chance crossed the threshold and took Pauline in his arms. He held her close until she could hold her pain no longer and she wept. From deep within she felt a release of long pent-up pain. She took Chance's hand and walked outside. There was enough pain in the house; she didn't need to dump another load there to be absorbed by she and her mother later.

They walked, hand-in-hand and in silence, for a long while. Eventually the walking turned into talking and Pauline did something she had never done before. She told Chance everything. She told him about her insecurities, her fears, life growing up under Biggie's roof, and the embarrassment she felt most of her life at the circumstances she had no control over. She shared her uncertainties about moving forward from this loss and what support she needed to be for her mother.

Chance listened, like Pauline listened to him when she was providing therapy. He asked her about her wishes and dreams. Pauline struggled to identify them, not because the grief and confusion overwhelmed her but because she had never been encouraged to identify and nurture them. Unlike Chance, she didn't grow up believing that she could be and do anything. She was stunted.

"Hey Pauline, did you enjoy living in the city?" Chance was trying to help her explore options and desires.

"It was no different from being here, except I worried about my parents more. I mean, I didn't go out; I worked and worked some more. I rented a room from a classmate, packed my lunches, ate frozen dinners at night. Actually, I probably like it here better. It's more familiar and if Mom needs me, I'm close."

"Do you want to keep working as a PTA?"

"Yeah, I enjoy making my own money and helping people. Jackson has enough clients around here that I could stay busy."

After chatting through some scenarios, they walked back to Pauline and Loretta's house.

Chance offered to take them out for dinner, but they were still working their way through casseroles left by church ladies.

"You can surely stay and eat with us, if you like." Loretta was not accustomed to having guests in the house and was tentative in her invitation.

"Thank you, Loretta but I've got a heap of work to do over at Old Tom's place.. well, at my place, I should say."

"So you came to an agreement, did you?" Pauline hadn't heard that a resolution had been reached but she was sure it was a great opportunity for Chance, even if an interim step to something else.

"We did. Pauline, I've got some things I want to talk to you about but I can imagine how drained you are today. Can I take you to breakfast in the morning?"

"That would be great. I don't have any clients until afternoon and I could use a change of scenery."

"Great, see you at eight tomorrow morning then." Chance leaned in and gave her a kiss on the cheek. "See you, Loretta. Take care now."

After the door closed behind Chance, Loretta looked at her beautiful daughter. "Honey, that boy loves you in a way I've never seen before, expect maybe between his mom and dad. How does it feel to be loved like that?"

Pauline had no words. She shrugged and spent the rest of the day contemplating her mother's words. She did feel loved, in a way she had never before experienced.

Chance walked up to the Whyte's house just as Pauline opened the front door.

"Good morning beautiful." He took her hand and pulled her close. "It looks like you got some good rest."

"I did. Thanks, and thanks for listening to my blubbering yesterday. I've never done that before, but it sure felt good. My head is so much clearer today."

"That's wonderful. Happy to be your sounding board." Chance opened the pickup door and Pauline slid along the seat.

Chance climbed into the driver's seat. Unless you knew about his shoulder surgery, you wouldn't know about his accident and the restrictions he previously lived under.

"You're doing really well with your shoulder, aren't you?" Pauline lost track of his recovery when she stopped providing his therapy services.

"Yes, it's so much better than I imagined it could be. After I stopped trying to do too much and paced myself, I started healing better. So, would you mind going to the city for breakfast? I really want a change of scenery for this conversation."

"Sure, that's fine. I don't have clients until this afternoon. I have to be honest though. I'm hungry, so can we do something more than a coffee shop?"

"Yes. I'm famished myself. There's a Dakota Marketplace restaurant that's great."

"Sounds good to me."

The hour drive to the restaurant passed quickly. They caught up on small talk, projects at Old Tom's place, the dude ranch and Chance's family activities. By the time they arrived at the restaurant and were seated, they were both ready to eat.

Chance ordered a mimosa for each of them. When the drinks arrived, he raised his glass. He clinked glasses with Pauline and smiled. "To us."

"Pauline, I'm not good at beating around the bush so I'm just going to say what's on my mind, okay?"

"I wouldn't expect anything different from you." Butterflies rolled around in her stomach.

"Pauline Whyte, I'm in love with you."

Pauline choked on her sip of mimosa.

"Well, I'm not sure what to make of that sputtering over there, but I am in love with you and I want to make a life with you." He rattled on, seemingly afraid to stop. "I know this might seem sudden to you but from the first day you came to work with me I knew that I wanted to be with you. I went through a rough patch there and I know it felt like I pushed you away but I worked through that and it had nothing to do with you. I am glad that you stopped being my therapist, not because you're not wonderful at your job but I knew you would never consider me as anything but a patient while you were working with me. I have Old Tom's place now. I know it's not as nice as Buffalo Ridge Ranch but I have a vision that I think will make it something special. I would love for you to be my partner in this enterprise."

Pauline watched Chance, animated, the words pouring out of him like they had been bottled up for a long time. He didn't take his eyes off her during the entire monologue. She squirmed in her seat. She had never been the recipient of such attention or outpouring of love and excitement to be with her.

"Why me, Chance?" He was her first boyfriend, the first man she spent time with exclusively. She had poor role models for a happy, loving marriage and although she saw the Davies family love, it still seemed foreign to her. She saw what her mother went through, being a Native American woman, and the defenses Biggie mounted if anyone even suggested that Loretta was less than a wonderful wife.

"Oh, Pauline, there are so many reasons. First, you are beautiful inside and out. Your heart is just as pure and kind as your smile and your eyes. We have fun together. You have shared things with me that showed me your soul and the depth of your goodness. My family adores you. You are smart and witty and, did I say beautiful? You are so beautiful."

"But, I've never been with a man, you know, intimately, and I know you've had all those buckle bunnies and you had girlfriends in high school. What if I don't measure up?"

Chance reached across the table and took her hands in his. He looked into her dark eyes. "I have absolutely no concerns about us being compatible like that. There are so many areas where we are totally in sync that I believe we will be there, as well."

"Chance, are you asking me to marry you?"

"Well, I would love nothing more, but I didn't want to scare you off by being too bold all in one day. So I thought, if it's ok with you, we could spend more intense time together. I am being inducted into the bull rider's hall of fame and I would like for you to come to Fort Worth with me for the ceremony. We could spend a few days driving there and exploring along the way and really spend more time together. As you said, I've been around quite a bit and I've been hopping from venue to venue chasing my rodeo dreams. Those days are behind me and I'm ready to settle down but I want you to be comfortable and confident that I'm somebody you want to be with for the rest of your life."

Pauline dabbed at tears welling in her eyes. Nobody had ever professed love for her like Chance did. The attention overwhelmed her and she felt as if she couldn't catch her breath. She understood within herself that it was foreign territory she'd been thrust into and, while she enjoyed her time with Chance, she had never considered a long-term partnership in the way he presented it. She just hadn't gone there yet. Her mind was racing, wondering what to do, how she really felt. Then, she remembered what her mom had said about Chance loving her in a special way. Pauline just hadn't allowed herself to consider it. Chance was the popular boy, and she was the wallflower. She had to pinch herself to make sure she wasn't dreaming.

"When is this trip?" she blurted out.

"Well, I didn't get much warning that they nominated me. It's coming up in two weeks. My parents will take the RV. They have reserved a table for the whole family. That's one thing about our family; we try to support one another as best we can. I know you don't have any brothers or sisters so it might seem a little over-whelming or intrusive to have so many people interested in what you're doing all the time, but I have appreciated their support over the years."

"So, is the whole family going to be there? Your sister too? Will Bella and Marco be coming?"

"Yes, that's the plan right now, except Marco will probably stay home with Jennifer. Steve arranged for someone to cover the dude ranch for the weekend. Dad has someone to do chores and Stella is flying in from Arizona. We won't all be together the whole time, just for the day of the ceremony and any other time we want to meet up with them. For Steve, Bella, Stella and

Jesse it will be a quick trip. They are all flying. Mom and Dad will take two or three days to get there, spend the weekend down there and then drive back. If you're up for it, I thought we could spend a little more time on the road."

"What about Old Tom? Who will be there to help him?"

"Tom is holding his own right now. He has neighbors who check in on him from time to time to see that he has plenty of food. I hired Justin Bowles to feed the livestock and check in everyday. Tom would like to come to the event but decided he is more comfortable staying close to home. He is encouraging me to go. And by the way, he adores you. The times you've been out to the place to help me, he has enjoyed visiting and getting to know you."

"Oh, really? He's a nice guy and I think he was probably good to my dad in the past, giving him jobs sometimes." Pauline fell silent, wondering what Biggie would think of Chance's confession of his feelings for her. She knew it would thrill Loretta to hear of the morning's conversation.

"Chance, I would like to go. I don't think though, that I'm comfortable being away from work for more than a week. Is that enough time to do what you want to do?"

"That's plenty of time to see if you can tolerate me for several days in a row." He smiled at her and reached across the table to caress her cheek. "Thank you, Pauline for being willing to give me this chance to show you how much I care for you and how right for each other I think we are."

The waitress brought their breakfast. Pauline's stomach was bouncing around with anxiety and excitement. She ate little of her meal although it was tasty.

"You haven't eaten much. Are you okay? I hope I haven't overwhelmed you with all my words. You should see my journal you gave me. There are about a dozen versions of this conversation. None of which look like how it went this morning. I'm sorry if I came on strong but, Pauline, you are the most wonderful thing that has ever happened to me and I was bursting at the seams to tell you."

"For me, this is a lot to take in. You know I've never been as close to a man as I am with you. I've told you things I have never shared with anyone, not even my mother, and in that way I feel very close to you. I love being around your family. They are so grounded and real."

Pauline had not yet told Chance that she loved him. For her, love had always been a twisted sort of beast that could deliver a back-hand as readily as a pat on the head. She had a lot of insecurities about being 'good enough' for Chance and knew she had to work through those. Fortunately, she had spent a lot of time alone and developed a meditation practice that helped her be quiet and work through her issues.

"So, how formal is this event?" They were returning to Buffalo Ridge and Pauline was planning the packing in her mind.

"Oh, it's not real formal. I'll wear jeans and a vest. Women wear jeans or skirts or whatever you want. No formal gowns or anything. We're just a bunch of guys who sit on sweaty bulls. Nothing fancy."

Pauline decided that she would reach out to Bella and Yvette to see what they planned to wear. She wasn't a western wear girl, other than jeans, so she needed to buy something special.

"Does your mom know about me going?"

"My mom knows everything. That's something about my mom. It's like she's psychic. She knows what I'm thinking even before I do. She's been saying for weeks that you are perfect for me and I knew it. I just, well, like I said, didn't want to scare you off by being too forward too soon. Even this, you may think, is too soon. Bella is the same. Since she met you she's told me how much she likes you and what a great addition you would be to the family."

The pickup pulled into Pauline's driveway and stopped. Chance reached for Pauline and drew her in for a deep kiss and a snug hug.

"Pauly, I'm so excited that you are going with me and we get to spend more time together! In the next couple weeks I want to see you as much as you're up for. I'll be working, but we can get in some dinners or something and I know Mom and Bella would love to see you at the ranch. Mom has said she would like for Loretta to come out too. Do you think she would be interested?"

Being called Pauly didn't irritate her the way it did when he was her patient. Now, it seemed a term of endearment.

"I think she would appreciate the invitation. She has a new chapter to write in her life now that Dad is gone and she's a little lost."

"Well let's plan something for this week. I'll talk to Mom when I get home and send you a text. Are there any evenings that are not good for you or Loretta?"

"No, I think this week we could make any evening work. Thanks Chance, for thinking of her, especially now."

"I'm just nice like that. You'll see." Chance

gave her a wink and a kiss on the cheek before he climbed back in his pickup.

Loretta was working and Pauline had work of her own to do in the afternoon. In the evening, when they were both together, Pauline summarized her conversation with Chance.

"Honey, I told you he loved you!"

"But Mom, do you think he's a good guy for me? You know I haven't dated."

"Oh honey, I'm sorry you did not have the opportunity to date when you were younger. Your dad, he was always so worried about you and he didn't want to take any chances that some guy wouldn't be good to you. Chance is a wonderful man, and he comes from such a good family. If you have any doubts, take some time and date others. But honestly, I think he's wonderful and you light up when he's around."

"I do? I guess I don't notice that."

"Oh, yes, you do. You just have to think about him or read a message from him and you're smiling. You've had some good times working with him at Old Tom's place and visiting the ranch. I've never seen you so happy."

Pauline nodded. She hadn't thought about it before, but now that her mother pointed it out, she knew it was true. She was happier than she had ever been.

"What do you think about taking this trip with him? Are you concerned that it's too much time alone with him?" Loretta had been with Biggie every minute that she or he wasn't working. They were comfortable being in one another's space. Loretta didn't know if Pauline had that ability…to just be with someone for hours and days on end.

"I'm willing to try it. I can see myself needing some time alone, since I'm alone now much of the time. I'll just have to make that happen if I need it. Oh, and Mom, they want us to come out to the ranch one night this week for dinner. I said I thought you would like to go. What do you think?"

"That would be lovely. You know I miss your dad, but it is nice not to have someone to take care of all the time and you know I have always admired that family."

"Okay, I will confirm when I get the day and time from Chance." Pauline paused and thought quietly for a moment. "Mom, thank you for being here and listening to me. This is all new to me and I appreciate your insights."

"I'm so glad you feel you can share with me Pauline."

17

———

The two weeks before the road trip to Fort Worth were busy. Pauline worked with her patients, and transitioned them to a self-guided home treatment plan for the week that she would be away. In her free time, she worked with Chance at Old Tom's place. Tom asked her to go through things with him inside the house. He donated or discarded old clothes, broken furniture, extra dishes and cookware.

"Thank you again, Pauline, for helping me out here. It's nice to have someone else to help me sort through this junk and decide what's got some use left in it and what needs to go. Besides, maybe one day you will be the woman of the house here and you'll have a better place to start from than having all this junk clutter up the cupboards."

Pauline looked at Tom, smiled and shrugged her shoulders. "I don't know Tom. I'm still feeling my way through all this."

"That Chance, he's a great guy. And he's crazy about you."

"Yes, he is a great guy."

"I'm just sorry I can't join you down there to Fort Worth. No bull rider deserves the hall of fame more than Chance. That man gave his all for nearly two decades to that sport. I'm so proud of him."

"Chance and I am sorry too, Tom. I know how much you poured into Chance's success and he does too. We'll bring back some pictures to share with you."

"Yeah, that would be great. I go back a long time with some of the old guys you'll meet there."

Pauline was sad for Tom that he wasn't well enough to travel and see his old friends one last time, as well as celebrate with Chance. It reminded her of something Biggie said repeatedly, before he got too sick to talk. He used to say that getting old isn't for sissies. Pauline had witnessed some hard battles lost by community elders over the past year, and was mindful that she didn't want to let life pass by without living it to the fullest.

LORETTA JOINED Pauline and the Davies family for dinner one night. Yvette hosted at their house and served her famous lasagna and garlic bread, a staple in the Davies house. Over the years, it fed sports teams, choirs, rodeo crews and more. Loretta enjoyed the evening and especially enjoyed being around Marco. He entertained her with his stories about school and ranch life. She could hardly believe that he had lived in the city until about six months prior.

As Pauline was driving home after a fun evening of laughing and storytelling, she was curious. "So Mom, how did you enjoy your evening?"

"You would do well, Pauline, to be part of that family. They are so loving and so much fun. I don't know when I've ever laughed so much."

It surprised Pauline to hear her mother be so affirmative in her opinion. She was always so reserved and usually held her thoughts close. Or maybe, Pauline considered, she hadn't asked for her opinion through the years.

THE DAY of the road trip finally arrived. Packing had been easy after talking with Bella and Yvette. Pauline bought a new shirt and earrings with some bling to wear to the event, and tucked them into a backpack with some casual clothes. Her stomach quivered as she hugged her mom farewell and climbed into Chance's pickup.

"I can't believe you got everything you need into one backpack. That's not enough for some women to get through dinner, let alone a week on the road." Chance looked at Pauline and smiled. He reached across the bench seat and covered her hand with his. "But, come to think of it, I can believe it. There's nothing typical about you, beautiful. How are you feeling?"

"Honestly, Chance, I'm nervous. This is all new to me. I've always been a loner and, well, to be together all day, every day will be different."

"I get it. It may seem like I'm a party boy, but the truth is I spent lots of hours driving alone, living in hotels alone and eating meals alone. You'll have your own room, and if you feel crowded and need some space during the day, just let me know. Okay?"

Pauline looked up at Chance and smiled. "You've got it. Thanks. Now, would you mind terribly if we stopped for a chai latté for me and coffee for you before we leave town? One last taste of Buffalo Ridge for the road?"

"You read my mind and…" Chance patted the thermos on the seat between them. "For good measure, I thought we could get the thermos filled. As you might guess, Mom sent a bag of food, but that won't stop us from stopping whenever you want to grab a warm bite to eat, okay?"

"Sounds good."

Pauline settled in for the ride, opening herself up to all the potential good that could come from this journey. They rode for several hours after fueling with coffee. They filled the hours with talk about the scenery, people and places they knew or had heard about, loud singing to favorite songs on the radio and spells of silence where each smiled to themselves. By late afternoon they were in the middle of Kansas looking for a place to stay for the night and a recommendation for good local cuisine. They took up a recommendation for a steak house and had a fabulous meal. After dinner they returned to the hotel and Chance walked Pauline to her room.

"I had a great day. I hope you did too." Chance leaned against the wall, smiling into Pauline's face.

"I really did. I think this will be a great trip. Thank you so much for choosing me, Chance." She reached up and kissed him good night.

As she lay in bed reviewing the day, Pauline was happy in a way she had never experienced. The time went fast, and she did not feel closed in. Her heart was full and the quiver in her stomach was long gone. She called her mom, as she promised she would, to check in and assure her she was safe and well.

"So, did you have a good day, honey?"

"Yeah, Mom. It really was a good day. I'm tired. I didn't sleep well last night so it feels great to stretch out on this big bed, watch some television and get a good night's sleep."

"That sounds nice. I hope you sleep well and continue to have a good trip. Things are quiet here. It's not so busy now that tourist season is over. A couple of the church ladies are taking me out to lunch tomorrow so I have that to look forward to."

"That's wonderful, Mom! I hope you have a good time."

"It will be a nice distraction. Well, rest up and I will talk to you tomorrow. Love you Pauline."

"Thanks Mom, I love you, too."

Pauline slept well that night and each night

of the trip. They spent two days in Oklahoma City exploring the area. With Pauline's agreement, they had dinner one night with rodeo friends of Chance. Pauline enjoyed listening to the rodeo stories and meeting Matt and Shelly. They were a little older than Chance and Pauline, and had two grade-schoolers. Matt retired from rodeo and they were both teaching now and operated a small ranch outside of Oklahoma City.

"Matt and Shelly have to be the sweetest people I have ever met." Pauline shared her thoughts as they rode back to the hotel after dinner.

"Aren't they amazing? Their faith has brought them through a lot over the years. Matt had some riding injuries and one year he was in a terrible accident. A semi clipped his trailer. He was just outside Los Angeles after making a good showing at an event there. He was on his way home to help Shelly take care of their daughter, Angela."

"Oh, I only heard them mention Kelsey and Kade, I didn't realize they had a third child."

"Yeah, poor Angela was their first baby. She had a rare cancer and died before her second birthday. It was a horrible time. It was about a month before she died that Matt was in this accident. The accident totaled his truck and trailer, and he lost his two best horses. He broke his pelvis and was laid up for a long time. Shelly had her hands full."

"I can't even imagine how hard that must have been for them. You would never know that they had such a tragedy, seeing them today, telling stories and just being so kind."

"Yeah. They are amazing and that's why whenever I get to these parts, I make it a point to spend some time with them. I really admire them and, I could tell they like you a lot."

"Is that so? How can you tell?"

"It's easy. Matt told me so when we were saying goodbye. He said he had never seen me so happy and relaxed and it looked good on me. He attributed it all to you."

"Well now, isn't that sweet? I agree, you are so much more relaxed than when I first met you after your accident."

"Oh, honey, that was a terrible time. The accident threw my whole life in the air like a bag of confetti, and I felt a lot of pressure to take all those pieces and puzzle them together to make a new life for myself. Then, as you know, my head and my body weren't working so well."

"Well, what do you think was the turning

point, when you knew you would come out of it and be okay?"

"Honestly? It was the day you told me I got a second chance to do something with my life. That I had a great career that ended with a win, and with it I got a lot of lessons that would carry me forward into a new and better life. I wouldn't have chosen that accident to make me start over, but it happened and I needed to pick myself up and move on. It helped a lot to know that you believed that I could, that I hadn't scrambled my head too much to come up with a plan, and that my body would eventually heal and be able to work hard again. It wasn't long after that you asked me to go to the rodeo and we ran into Old Tom. All those pieces came together within a matter of days and you were at the center of it all. You stole my heart then, Pauline Whyte."

They had reached the hotel and were sitting in the parking lot, breathing in the essence of each other.

"Thank you, Pauline, for coming along on this trip. It means a lot to me. I can't share my bull riding life with you, since that's in the past, but it's a treat to have you by my side for the hall of fame ceremony. That's like the icing on a very rich cake." Chance slid across the seat to get closer to Pauline and wrapped his arms around her.

"It is my pleasure. I am a little sad that I didn't know you before, but I guess all happens as it's meant to and here we are." Pauline rested her head on Chance's shoulder. They sat together until the chill in the air enticed them inside the hotel.

"Hey, how about a swim? I think it would be good therapy for me. What do you say?"

"Sounds like a great way to finish this wonderful evening together."

The following day, they met up with Yvette and Dan in Fort Worth. It was the day before the big event. Pauline and Yvette had their nails done and shopped, a gift of pampering from Yvette. The guys went to the venue site to see if there were any old-timers there to chat with and pass on Old Tom's well-wishes. They found three fellas that knew Tom and passed along their greetings. Dan had met two of the cowboys before and the older cowboys had followed Chance over his career.

"Son, it's the cowboy's life to run into the wall and come out clean on the other side. You look like you've mended up pretty well. What will you be doing now?" James Porter was a bull rider from way back and served on the board of directors for the bull rider's association.

"Yeah, James, I really have healed up well. Once in a while my head still tricks me and my shoulder aches a bit but those are little things compared to where I've been. Truth be told, I'm taking over Old Tom's riding school. I'm partnering with my brother who has a dude ranch and we're bringing in some longer schools for elite training. I've also got a talented young equine therapist who will give lessons to some kids who seem to do well with the horses. I'll run some cattle and plant some crops there at Tom's. It's enough for me right now, though I do hope to expand some day."

"That sounds like a great plan. Think you'll settle down with a woman soon? It's hard to find that special one living on the road, but now, maybe you'll have more time to do some courting." Archie Blevins, another of the old cowboys chimed in.

"I'm working on that now. In fact, Pauline came to town with me and you can meet her tomorrow night."

"Well, I'll be. You sure have wasted no time moving on. Good job there, Chance." Archie reached out to shake Chance's hand.

"In fact, mom took her out for a girls date

and it's getting close to time for us to meet up for dinner. What do you say, Dad, should we head out?"

Dan checked his watch. "Son, you are right on the money. It was sure good to see you good men. You all take care now and we'll see you tomorrow night." The group exchanged handshakes and well wishes until they would meet up again the following night.

As Dan and Chance walked to the pickup Dan put his arm around his son. "You know Chance, it must feel pretty good to be in the company of great men like those fellas. Those boys beat a lot of odds to ride out their careers and become Hall of Famers. I'm real proud of you."

"I'm still pinching myself to see that I'm not dreaming. Thank you for coming down to celebrate with me, Dad. It means a lot. You and Mom have been so supportive over my career, practically turning me over to Old Tom and then coming to so many of my events. I love you guys."

"We love you too, son."

18
____

The Davies family made a great showing at the hall of fame induction event. They stood to cheer for Chance when he received his award, while the video of his last ride played in the background. Chance delivered an acceptance speech that brought the Davies family table to tears. Pauline had secretly videotaped Old Tom congratulating Chance on his accomplishments over the years. He wove in stories of the early years when Chance spent every available hour working with Tom to develop his skills. Tom concluded the video with tearful congratulations and well wishes to his long-time friends in the association.

Chance introduced each family member and

Pauline, calling her his super-special girlfriend who brought more healing and vision to his world than he ever knew possible. It was a moving ceremony, branded on the minds of the Davies family and Pauline for eternity. The family gathered at a nearby lounge after the event to spend time together before they all scattered the following day.

"Hey bro, I'm real proud of you. You're one heck of a cowboy." Stella looked at their brother Jesse and the two of them started reciting a cowboy poem with rap overtones. It was a funny poem about life as an eight-second junkie living on adrenaline and fast food chasing the prize from city to city. They had the group laughing hysterically with the images portrayed in the poem.

Steve and Bella gave Chance an outstanding memory book they had published. It held photos and news clippings collected from his years on the circuit, quotes from mentors, teammates, competitors and others.

Chance was touched and close to tears. "Thank you. You all must have worked fast to get this done. It's fantastic."

"Yes. You didn't give us much warning but between Bella and Mom, they put that book together in no time and with rush delivery, well… there it is."

Dan and Yvette gifted Chance a small collection of livestock for the riding school.

Pauline gave him a copy of Old Tom's congratulatory comments with a classy CD cover to commemorate the event.

"I can't believe you… well, yes, I can. You are sneaky! I must remember that. All that time I thought you were working with Tom on the house you were making this. I will cherish this forever." Chance leaned in and gave Pauline a kiss.

"Well, this has been one great party but it's not over yet."

Chance stood up, reached in his pocket and dropped to one knee in front of Pauline. There, in a lounge in Fort Worth, before his entire family, including Bella, Chance asked Pauline to marry him.

"I realize I'm jumping the gate here, Pauline." He turned to the family and explained that the road trip was a test run, and because it was not finished yet he really hadn't allowed the test case to run its course. "I just knew, while you girls were out pampering yourselves yesterday, that was my only window to go with Pops here and find this special ring. I realize this is risky, asking you here on this special day in front of all these people. I want to assure you I called your mom already and asked for your hand. She was excited and said yes immediately, which I hope you will too. Pauline, will you marry me?"

Chance opened the box and held it out so Pauline could see the stunning two carat round diamond raised above a wide white gold band etched with graceful filigree scroll. The group got quiet; the women sucked in their breath and held it, waiting for Pauline to give her response.

Pauline looked at the ring. Tears of joy filled her eyes. She looked at Chance and answered. "Yes Chance, I will marry you…" Then, waving her hand toward the group she added "And your family!"

The group cheered while Chance took the ring and placed it on her finger.

"Oh Chance, it's so beautiful!"

Chance took her face in his hands, looked deep into her eyes and responded. "You are the beauty, Pauline."

Dan handed Pauline his phone. Her mother was on video chat on the phone and offered congratulations.

"Oh Mom, thank you so much. I guess we have a lot to talk about when I get back." Pauline and Loretta laughed and agreed they would have some planning to do when she returned to Buffalo Ridge.

Jesse and Stella teased Steve about making his relationship with Bella permanent. Bella blushed and told the crowd they were in no rush. Turning the attention back to Pauline and Chance, she congratulated them and said she would be available to do catering. Steve offered up the dude ranch as a venue.

"Well, thank you all. This is really fresh and Chance and I, and my mom, have a lot of talking to do before we nail anything down. I still don't have my feet on the ground! It may be days before it really hits me. This was such a surprise." Pauline gently stroked her ring while smiling at Chance and the rest of the group.

"I bet you have a good start on your plans by the time you get back to the ranch. Chance, when do you think you'll be moving out to Old Tom's?"

"Ready for me to move on, eh Mom?" Chance laughed.

"No, I just wanted to be available to help if you need it."

"Honestly, I think as soon as we get back I need to move the RV over there and spend most of my time over there. He's not well and I want to get as many of the repairs and things done as

I can before spring comes. I hope to be busy with bull riding school starting in early spring."

"That makes sense. We'll have the RV home about the same time you get there and I'll get it cleaned up right away for you."

"Thanks Mom. I would like to raise a toast to our parents, the reason we exist and have become the wildly successful people we are."

"Here, here" rang through the lounge as they toasted Yvette and Dan, who kissed in front of the group.

"Well, you know we are proud of all of you and are so grateful to celebrate occasions like this double-whammy tonight. Here's to many more celebrations. In fact, I think you, Jesse, have something to share with the group, don't you?" Dan liked to draw out their youngest son who often sat silently, enjoying himself but sharing little.

"Gee, thanks Dad. Uh, well, most of you have followed Kerry and I as we've found and lost and found ourselves again over the past few years. Next weekend there's a big fundraiser for Albert Harnisch. Well, let me back up and guys, nobody knows anything about this yet so please, mum's the word." He paused while the heads around the table nodded. "So last week I went to talk with Mr.

Braun, Kerry's dad, and asked him for her hand."

There was clapping and smiles from the group. "Not so fast. I have to pass a challenge before he'll give me permission."

"Seriously? What's the challenge?" Stella was curious now about where this was going.

"You'll like this, Stella. At the fundraiser next week, I have to perform a cowboy poem. I couldn't use any old poem; I had to write a new one. Anyway, if my performance passes Mr. Braun's test, I can ask Kerry to marry me. And you're all invited to this. It's at the new veterinarian office I'm building on the old McHenry place as a surprise for Kerry."

"Man, you've been doing all this behind our backs? We could have been helping you." Steve shifted in his seat, uncomfortable to know he had not lent his baby brother, who had helped him so much, a hand with his new adventure.

"You all have so much going on, and honestly, it's been very therapeutic for me. I feel like I have something substantial to offer her and a hand up as she comes back to the community as a new veterinarian. Anyway, after the fundraiser a bunch of folks are heading out to the new clinic building and I will drive Kerry home, but stop off there and surprise her. I will also propose to her there. So you're all invited. Stella, I realize you're going back to Arizona and I would love to have you there but the cows are calling."

"That's right, but man, I would love to have a video of all these activities."

"You think she will say yes?" Chance reached over and gave his little brother a shove.

"I sure hope so. I see you two so happy here and Mom and Dad are so happy. I want that for Kerry and I too."

"Of course she will say yes. Pauline, you probably haven't gotten to know Kerry much, or maybe you knew her in school, but I think you will all get along really well."

"I remember her as being super smart and very nice. I'm so happy for you, Jesse." Pauline reached out to shake Jesse's hand. She was grateful to have the attention focused somewhere other than on her. "I guess after all this we will coordinate dates so we're not stepping all over each other's plans."

"Yeah, I'm sure all you women will get together and plan everything. Just let us guys know so we show up on the right day." Jesse was not genuinely cavalier about the planning; he wanted to defer planning until he passed the test and had an acceptance to his proposal.

"My heart is full. Here's to our wonderful

and growing family." Yvette held her nearly empty wine glass up for a final toast. The group lingered as long as they dared, with early flights out of the city for some coming in a few hours. They said their final goodnights and congratulations and went off to their respective sleeping quarters.

Chance and Pauline, although up late the night before, rose early and met for breakfast. They were both eager to get on the road and move forward to their next chapter.

"I can't believe you did that last night, Chance!"

"Oh, why not? Did you think about saying no to my proposal in front of my entire family?"

"No. I just mean that it was your night, a celebration of your success and your hard work. It didn't need to be about me too."

"Oh, my dear, my life is about you and making you happy. I dedicate my days to building the best life possible for the two of us. I don't mean mansions and fancy cars. I mean a genuine sit down to eat dinner, raise a family, be happy, every day in love and life."

They filled the rest of the journey home with joy as they talked about improvements at Old Tom's place, soon to be their new home, Jesse and Kerry's big news, the enterprise they could build using the indoor arena and growing the rodeo school and therapy services.

By the time they reached Buffalo Ridge they were ready to talk with Loretta and get her input on their wedding plans. Pauline wanted simple and small. She never was one to feel showy and did not enjoy being the center of attention. The beautiful engagement ring stunned Loretta. Pauline and Chance had gone to the jewelers before leaving Fort Worth and bought the equally stunning matching wedding bands.

THE FOLLOWING few weeks were spent in celebration, working at Old Tom's place, and joining Jesse and Kerry for their surprise party and engagement. Yvette invited the women - Bella, Pauline and Loretta, Kerry and her mother - to lunch to start the conversation about wedding plans and to celebrate the growing family.

Pauline greeted Bella with a hug and whispered in her ear, "I wish we were celebrating you too."

Bella whispered back, "In due time we will be. I am certain of that and that's just fine with me."

Pauline smiled at her and nodded in understanding before turning her focus back to the conversation about her own nuptials. She happily announced, "We will have a spring wedding. It's a time of renewal and growth and a perfect time to start a new life."

EPILOGUE
STELLA

 $\mathcal{N}$ early a year ago Stella sat beside Chance's bed, praying silently that he would emerge from his coma, scared that he would wake but have serious brain damage. She sat tall and strong, a fencepost for her parents to lean on. It would have crushed them to lose one of the Davies brood. Heck, they cried when they lost a good horse or a pregnant cow.

Today, she was back in Buffalo Ridge helping Yvette and Bella prepare for Chance and Pauline's wedding. Getting to this point, with the wedding in just three days, was a series of negotiations. Chance wanted a huge celebration, the way he lived life on the circuit. He wanted all his rodeo buddies from around the globe to come to Buffalo Ridge. Pauline wanted to keep it small and simple, just family and a few close friends. To keep the peace, Stella and Bella took over the planning, with the couple's blessings. They planned for a smallish and classy to-do with lots of beautiful flowers, courtesy of Steve's greenhouse. Bella worked with them to develop a fantastic menu. Yvette snuck a few extra guests on the list, but honestly, on the day of, what were they going to do, refuse to get married if there were extra guests?

"If it were me getting married, I'd be riding to the mesquite tree altar at the fork of Spiney and Smolder Trails in Bridal Veil Canyon on a horse, away from people, with sage bushes as my bouquet and grazing cattle our witnesses." Stella preferred to be working cattle on the trail, spending nights under the stars at the edge of a campfire, and the occasional cowboy poet's gathering.

Stella hadn't considered marriage after being abandoned by Hank, a no-good cowboy who abandoned her in New Mexico. She avoided men, unless there was a cow between them and a rope in her hand. That is, until he appeared.

Brandon Cage left his family ranch and pursued his dream of being a lawyer for the people. A handsome, well-to-do bachelor, he attracted a lot of beautiful women but they didn't catch his eye the way Stella did. She was beautiful, hard working, kind-hearted, intelligent, and ran a successful cattle operation. She possessed all the attributes he desired in a partner, and he always got what he wanted.

Until he met Stella.

ACKNOWLEDGMENTS

Linda Zeppa, editor and intuitive writing coach extraordinaire, thank you for your patient guidance and support in all my writing endeavors.

ABOUT THE AUTHOR

Kim Smart was raised on the edge of the Badlands in western South Dakota, but *grew up* in Alaska after landing there as a young nurse. Two decades later, she moved to San Diego to attend law school. After graduating, she returned to Alaska to again work in health care, this time at the intersection with law and public service.

Kim has always had a diverse love for writing and reading, enjoying romance, women's literature, historical fiction, poetry, and stories of people living authentic lives. Following a lifelong dream, Kim has turned to writing. She currently writes romance, women's literature, and historical fiction, along with nonfiction articles for various publications.

When not writing or traveling, Kim enjoys time with her parents and extended family, hiking and creating in the kitchen. She presently lives in Arizona, or wherever the wind blows her as she visits her children, grandchildren, and other interesting parts of our world. She has much to write about and many stories to tell!

Join Kim at https://kimsmartauthor.com to get notification of new releases and exclusive reader giveaways. If you enjoyed this book, please leave a review.

ALSO BY KIM SMART

Buffalo Ridge Ranch Series

Falling for Home - Book 1

Jesse Davies had been in love with his hometown girl for as long as he could remember. As they drift apart, he searches for meaning in his life. To find love, he must first find his voice and find himself.

Kerry Braun had dreams larger than Buffalo Ridge. To pursue her dreams, she leaves everything behind. The pursuit to become a veterinarian consumes her, blocking out all opportunities for lasting love. Will she ever find her way back?

Can two small-town friends find happily-ever-after?

The first novel in Kim Smart's Buffalo Ridge Ranch series tugs at emotions as the dance of love tests the boundaries of happily-ever-after.

Two for Love - Book 2 (*Coming Spring 2020*)

Steve Davies lived his life in the shadow of his late

wife's dreams. To emerge from his grief, he must take a chance. Hoping to expand the dreams they had together, he starts a dude ranch. In the process, he hires a cook - a city girl who brings along her son.

Bella Giordano needed to find safety for her young son. On a whim, she moves them from Manhattan to the Badlands of South Dakota, hoping the small town life, away from mob threats and smog, will be good for them both.

Will grief dissolve and a new opportunity be enough to build a new family?

The second novel in Kim Smart's Buffalo Ridge Ranch series sets the table for new opportunities and the possibility of love. Will hurts heal and love grow?

DRESSING UP STELLA - BOOK 4 (*Coming Summer 2020*)

Stella Davies lived far away from Buffalo Ridge Ranch. Fearing repeat abandonment, she built the life of a cowboy nurturing her herd on the rugged edge of nature in Arizona. But to find happiness, she must face these fears. When she moves to the remote high desert, she is forced to face her fears.

Ranching was in Brandon Cage's blood, but a new career as a lawyer changed his focus. He buried himself in his new profession and totally ignored his heart's desires.

Do they have the gumption to clear the way to give love a chance? Will their love arrive in time to find a life happily-ever-after?

The fourth novel in Kim Smart's Buffalo Ridge Ranch series is about overcoming past hurts and prioritizing love.

Standalone Novels

Tangled Ribbons

The essences of individual humans are substantially more alike than they are different. Gertie Hall lives this truth as she rises from the young child of a Hitler's henchman to a world-renown advocate for human rights. Through scientific endeavors, humanitarian efforts and a tireless fight to right the wrongs of her father, she explores her feminine self, intellect, ingenuity, and grit.

A hole remains in her soul where two childhood friends were ripped away, and Gertie's own father was complicit in the disappearance of their families. *Tangled Ribbons*, scene by scene, captures the life of Gertie, intertwined with the stories of her friends, Sarah and Hannah, who flee fiery Berlin and establish new identities and new lives in far away places. Late in their lives, Gertie offers a heart-wrenching plea for amends and a new generation is enfolded in their healing.

Christmas Market Reunion

Brooke Linton, 26, is stuck in a rut, aggressively pursuing professional recognition in corporate Miami with little time for fun. She tries to convince herself that life is great, so long as she has a good job, family at Christmas and she can sing in the church choir.

A chance meeting with an American in Amsterdam gives Brooke a glimpse into what life could be like outside the office.

After returning from vacation, her professional world falls apart. Through soul searching and discussion with a sister, Brooke grows to see this as an opening to create a life of her dreams. Little did she know how far those dreams would take her.

This sweet, wholesome romance will surprise and delight you with world travel, unexpected encounters, and fairytale weddings. The question remains. Can a chance encounter on foreign soil turn into something more? Get Christmas Market Reunion today and lose yourself in happily ever after.